A Beauty to

A Beauty to his Beast 2:

An Urban Werewolf Story

By:

Natavia

SOUL PUBLICATIONS

Kanya

It had only been two weeks since I had my pups. My parents have been begging me for the address so they could come visit them, but I have been stalling. I have been sending them pictures, but I was afraid that they would find out what I am. After I fed the twins, I laid them down in their crib. They looked just like their father; they are going to be a handful when they get older.

I took a shower, got dressed, and applied a little make-up. My hair had grown out in a bushy mass of thick curls. Since I became a shifter, my hair began growing very fast. The hair cuts didn't last long. I wore a pair of skinny jeans; a fitted, black long-sleeve shirt; and on my feet were a pair of flats. Goon walked into the room. "Good-morning, beautiful," he said in a deep, raspy voice.

"Good-morning," I said to him, wrapping my arms around his neck. He picked me up then kissed my lips, slipping his tongue into my mouth.

"Get down, boy," I said to him laughing. Goon put me down with a smirk on his face. "Why do you talk to me like a misbehaved pet dog?" he asked me.

"You have been a bad boy," I said, patting his shoulder. Goon picked me up then tossed me over his shoulder. "I should spank your ass for your rude tongue," he said to me.

"Spank me, daddy," I said, wiggling my back side against his face. His canines sank into my right butt cheek.

"Damn it, Goon! Put me down before I get mad," I said to him.

"We haven't played in a while," he said, putting me down. I looked at his erection that grew down his leg. "The twins take a lot of energy out of me; I be too tired," I said to him.

This is some bullshit. My dick has been aching all week, Goon said to himself.

"I heard that," I said laughing at him.

"Go get some air. I'm going to stay here with the twins," he said to me. I kissed him good-bye then headed down the stairs. I missed Kofi a lot. It seemed like he had been gone forever. The house just didn't feel the same without him. I never thought that I would miss his orchestra music playing throughout the halls.

When I walked into the kitchen, Izra was drinking a pitcher of water. "It's too early for this bullshit," I said to him.

"Oh shut up, Kanya! What are you ready to do anyway? That nigga is letting you out of the house? You must have finally gave him some, didn't you? That nigga is starting to become aggressive," Izra instigated.

"None of your business. Now where is Adika? She and I are supposed to be shopping today."

"She's in the shower, and I didn't tell her she could go anywhere. Don't you become a bad influence on her because unlike you, she listens," Izra said.

I growled at him. "Cute, Kanya, really cute," he laughed. Adika walked into the kitchen glowing. She and Izra must have been having sex all night, which was the norm for them.

"Do you two ever stop fucking?" I asked them. Adika blushed with her head down, and Izra smirked. "What can I say? I'm a wild animal. I like fucking, especially in the trees," Izra stated. My mouth dropped, and then Adika punched his arm. "Would you stop telling all of our business?" Adika asked Izra.

"There are no secrets in the pack," Izra said chewing on raw broccoli.

Adika rubbed her hand over Izra's crotch. "You want to do it in front of Kanya?" he asked her as she smiled.

"WHAT THE FUCK!" Izra hollered, looking down in his sweat pants. Adika fell over laughing.

"Where is my dick?" Izra asked Adika.

"I made it disappear until Kanya and I come back," she said.

"I'm seriously jealous that you can do that," I said to Adika.

"Fucking witch!" Izra hollered as he continued to look down in his pants.

Amadi came into the kitchen. "What is going on in here?"

“This muthafucka made my dick disappear. Nigga, help me look for it.” Izra stated, and then all of us burst into laughter.

“Y’all think this shit is funny? I got two damn balls and nothing between it. You know how much my dick means to me. Where is Dayo? I know that nigga would help me find it. Then after he does, I would have to kill him,” Izra fussed.

“Baby, please make it come back. I swear I won’t tell our business. You can’t do this shit to me; it’s fucking up my manhood,” Izra pleaded, holding himself. Adika did something with her fingers. “Don’t play with me, Izra. That was a warning, and I heard that statement you made. You think I’m submissive? Well, think again because I am not to be fucked with.” Izra wasn’t listening to Adika; he was looking down his pants and feeling himself, making sure it was there.

“You shorted me an inch! I measured my dick, and the last time I checked it was twelve inches,” Izra fussed. Amadi shook his head then walked back out of the kitchen. I had seen all of them naked after shifting back to human form, and they all are big. When Goon and I mated, he grew a few more inches, and when I really thought about it, I couldn't understand how I took him.

"I'll give it back later," Adika said to Izra. He looked at her with his eyes turning red. I didn't understand why Izra's eyes were red. His canines protruded out of his mouth, his breathing sped up, then he cracked his neck.

"Don't fuck with me Adika," Izra warned with his face turning—he was shifting.

"Okay fine," she said, doing something else with her fingers. I still couldn't believe that Adika was a witch. Izra checked inside of his pants again then walked out of the kitchen.

"He loves his dick more than he loves anything else," Adika fussed as she and I walked out of the house. When I got inside of Goon's truck, Adika looked frustrated.

"Talk to me," I said to her.

"I really like Izra, but at times I don't think he cares about me; it's always about sex," Adika stewed.

"He is young. Izra still has a nineteen-year-old mind," I said to her.

"He fucks like a grown man, so he needs to start acting like one," Adika spat. She and I chatted until I pulled into the mall parking lot. When she and I got out of the truck, Keora was standing by the entrance, still disguised as the college girl.

"Why is she here?" I asked Adika.

"I want you two to get along. She is my sister, and you are my best friend. I understand that she and Goon fooled around, but that was ages ago, and he doesn't remember. It's stressing me out because I feel like I'm in the middle," Adika finally said.

"I came in peace Kanya," Keora said with a smirk on her face. Keora was the type of woman that made that inner bitch come out of you.

"Let's be honest, you had the dick before. I'm not being cordial with no woman who fucked my MATE," I said to her.

"I must be a real threat to you if you are jealous about the past. No matter what you say, I had him first," Keora said, getting mad.

"And I have him for eternity," I said to her.

"One thing about witch craft is that it has a mind of its own when it's provoked," Keora said.

"Can we all just get along?" Adika asked. I knew that our problems were wearing down on her, and it wasn't fair to her.

"I will be cordial with Keora for the time being," I said walking off. I ended up in the Victoria's Secret store. I was going to buy something nice for Goon tonight. After I gave birth, I healed immediately. Goon and I could've made love the day after if I wanted to, but I was drained. The twins took a lot out of me. When they were first born, they needed my milk almost every hour. Adika was going through the racks, and Keora was testing out the perfume.

"I like that one. Maybe you should get it in black. I can't wait for the surprise you have for me tonight," Goon's voice boomed in my head.

"Seriously? UGHHHHHHHH! What did I tell you about that? Why are you in my visions? Now my surprise is ruined," I spat.

"The twins are sleep and I'm bored. Amadi is making oils, Elle is fixing shit and Izra is just being Izra," he laughed.

"Can we do normal things sometimes, like using a cell phone?" I asked Goon. Keora was looking at me. I forgot that witches can hear your thoughts when they are close by.

"Do you mind?" I asked Keora.

"You are really crazy," Keora said laughing. Her laugh burned my ears and made me drop my items. She laughed even harder, making my head throb. The pressure made my nose bleed. Keora body flew against the wall; the costumers in the store started screaming.

"How did you do that?" I asked Goon.

"*I don't know. I just got mad and you felt it. Stay away from the crazy bitch, Kanya,"* Goon replied. I got some tissues out of my purse for my nose.

Adika looked at me and looked at Keora. "What happened?" Adika asked us while Keora was getting up off of the floor.

"Nothing, just a small nose bleed," I answered Adika.

After I paid for my items, I walked out of the store. As much as I wanted to understand where Adika was coming from, I couldn't do it. I was not going to be cordial with Keora. That sneaky witch was up to something. Adika rode with Keora, and I was somewhat glad that she did. It pained me that my friendship with Adika may not ever be the same.

When I got home, Dayo was sitting in the living room watching T.V. I didn't like his vibe, and I really wanted him gone.

"Good afternoon, Kanya, come and sit down for a second. I would like to talk to you," Dayo said to me. Goon came down the stairs. "You can talk to her when I'm present and only when I'm present," Goon said crossing his arms and leaning up against the living room entry way.

"I wanted to apologize for everything I have said," Dayo said. Goon growled at him, and then his eyes turned blue. "Goon, stop it!" I shouted.

"That's a bunch of bullshit," Goon spat, pacing back and forth.

"If you say so, bro. I just want to make peace with this pack. That's how Kofi raised us; we are one despite our downfalls. We are all family, and it's been that way for years," Dayo said standing up. Goon's mood softened up at the mention of Kofi. The bond he had with Kofi was stronger than a father and son bond.

"This house is big enough for you stay away from me. Your thoughts are sick. If it wasn't for Kofi and this brotherhood, I would've killed you in your sleep. Stay away from my mate too. Don't speak to her unless I'm there. If you disobey my rules, I will cast you out of this pack so you can starve to death." Goon said sending chills up my spine. He can be so loving, but then he can become another person. Dayo nodded his head then walked out of the living room.

"He is trying to make peace," I said to Goon.

"His thoughts are sick; he is not one of us. Kofi showed and taught us brotherhood within this pack. I cannot let that go to waste so that is the only reason for Dayo being here," Goon said.

Goon checked my face and my ears. I giggled. "What are you doing?" I asked him.

"Just making sure you're okay. I wanted to bite Keora's throat, but I had the twins," he said. Akea started screaming at the top of his lungs. I ran upstairs into our bedroom. I picked him up then rocked him while Kanye still slept peacefully.

"What's the matter, baby?" I asked him.

"He had a bad dream," Goon said, standing next to me rubbing his head.

"How do you know?"

"I saw it," Goon said sadly.

"What did you see?"

"A demon sacrificing his soul, but the dream was blurry," he said. My life almost drained out of my body. "How could a baby dream about that? Aren't they supposed to be playing with angels?" I cried.

"I don't know what that was about," Goon said taking Akea away from me, holding him securely in his arms. After Akea went back to sleep, I took a shower then got into bed. Goon was in front of the fireplace doing push-ups; his strong muscles flexed in his back and in his arms.

"The animal in you is drooling over me, but yet I still can't get any pleasure from you," he said doing pushups using one arm, not breaking a sweat.

"I'm worried about that dream," I said to Goon. He growled then stood up stretching his muscles out. "It was a nightmare and everybody has them. Who told you babies dream about angels?"

"Don't worry about it," I spat, turning over in bed. Goon got into bed and wrapped his arm around me. "I would not let anything harm our pups. I would sacrifice my life for them and you," he spoke into my ear. I pulled his arm around me. "I know you will," I said.

Goon

"What does it mean when a baby dream about demons?" I asked Elle after we came back from hunting.

"I don't know too much about demons, but they are tied to witches in a way. Ages ago, witches use to sacrifice themselves to demons to gain more power, to practice dark magic. I don't know if it's true, but that's what I have heard," Elle said.

Izra walked into the kitchen with an angry look on his face. "What's up, bro? What is the matter with you?" I asked Izra.

"Adika broke up with my black ass. She told me I only wanted to fuck her and wasn't interested in her feelings."

"Seriously, bro? You don't see what the problem is?" Elle asked Izra.

"No, I don't. I should be mad at her since she was fucking with my dick. Adika knows I like her, but I'm a wolf, and my sex drive is high."

"I'm not even trying to talk about sex. I haven't had pussy in weeks. I ate two deer yesterday because Kanya has been holding out on me," I told my brothers.

"ARRRGHHHHHHHHHHHHHHHH!" Kanya screamed.

"Damn it. She is getting those markings again," I told Izra and Elle.

I ran upstairs then down the hall. I charged into our bedroom. Kanya was on the floor with her fangs hanging out of her mouth. Her eyes were gold, and her face was changing into her jackals.

"It hurts!" she screamed. I picked her up then placed her into the shower to run cold water on her. She was getting more of my markings on her body. Every time she got one of my markings, she became stronger; her jackal was even bigger. Kanya was becoming me. She cut her finger the other day, and it closed up immediately. I was worried that my beast would become too much for her. My aggressiveness and my inability to control my anger will soon happen within her. I ripped her clothes off; the markings were forming down her arms.

"It hurts," she cried, digging her sharp nails into my arms.

"It's almost done. Just squeeze me tightly," I told her. After the markings appeared on her arms, her body went limp, but I caught her.

She started sniffing the air. "There is a deer a few miles away from this house," she said. Her body crouched down. Her neck transformed along with the bones in her body. I could see the hair piercing through her skin like needles. Seconds later, Kanya was gone, and her jackal was standing in her place in the bathroom with me. The sounds of her sniffing echoed throughout the bathroom. Kanya ran then jumped out of the bedroom window and into the woods.

"Damn it, Kanya! Elle is going to be pissed that you broke the window; he just fixed it last week," I said into her head.

"I had a burst of energy. Come and join me," she responded back.

When I turned around, Dayo was standing in the doorway to the bedroom. "Yo, like what the fuck are you standing there for? Didn't I tell you to stay the fuck away from me?" I asked him. My heart started beating fast as my beast wanted to attack him.

"The phone is for you," he said, tossing it to me. I caught the phone with my right hand.

"Speak!" I barked into the cordless phone.

"I'm looking for a Johnathan Simpson," the caller said. I was puzzled until I realized that was my fake name.

"Speaking," I answered.

"I believe you were looking for a building to open up your jewelry store. If you are still looking for the space, I think I found something," he said. I forgot that I contacted a realtor a week ago. I wanted to surprise Kanya. We had a lot of jewelry that's worth millions, most of the pieces even came from Ancient Egypt. Kanya stated that she wasn't used to just sitting around, so I wanted to give her something. She always said she wanted to own a business.

"How soon can you show it to me?" I asked him.

"Tomorrow around noon, how is that?"

"Cool, what's your name again?"

"Steven Mace, I will see you tomorrow around noon. Check your email. I just sent you the address. See you soon," he said, hanging up.

"Aye, nigga, are you trying to go to the club with me?" Izra asked me when I walked downstairs with the twins in my arms.

"I have to ask Kanya," I said. Amadi, Elle and Izra looked at me then started laughing.

"What's funny?" I asked them.

"Nigga, your life is what's funny! You are becoming human. You're trying to open up stores and shit," Izra said.

We heard the sounds of glass breaking and growling. Kanya came into the kitchen in beast form. "What the fuck is that?" Amadi asked, ready to shift.

"Kanya's jackal has gotten bigger," I said to them.

"She is becoming you?" Elle asked me.

"Yup, beast and all," I said. I honestly wasn't happy about that. I wanted Kanya to remain sweet and gentle like she was at first. Soon she will have my attitude. I know she is my soul mate, but I didn't think it would be this way. I didn't think when we became one, it would be literally.

Blood dripped from her mouth, and she licked her teeth then growled. "Yo, what the fuck is wrong with her? You think she got rabies?" Izra asked me. Kanya walked past me with her tail raised up; she was taunting me.

After she left out of the kitchen, everyone was quiet just staring at me. "You need to show her who is Alpha!" Elle said with Amadi and Izra agreeing with him.

"So, you think I'm losing my touch, huh?" I asked them.

"Nigga, you losing something! Kanya just burst through the window, and she got blood on the floor. Not only is she breaking house rules but she got her roles all screwed up. Look at you standing there holding your babies while your mate hunts. I think you are going soft on us, my nigga," Izra laughed.

"Two Goons under the same roof? I need a drink and perhaps some pleasure from a woman," Amadi said.

"Nigga, you wait years to finally realize that you need some pussy?" Izra asked Amadi.

"Would you shut the fuck up for a second?" I barked at Izra. Izra growled at me, and I growled back louder causing him to step back. "Don't fuck with me, little brother," I warned him.

"Seriously, Goon, Kanya is not supposed to be challenging you. She walked right past you with her tail raised up. Kanya's beast is a little too strong for her. I remember how you was when you first turned. You was uncontrollable. You even killed everyone on the slave plantation. She cannot have that behavior around the pups," Elle said with everyone else agreeing. I didn't know what to do at this point. Elle reached his arms out grabbing the twins from me. "Go and talk to her. It's going to get ugly. I would keep an eye on them," Elle said to me. Izra patted me on the back. "Good luck, my nigga."

When I walked into our bedroom, Kanya was applying lotion on her body. "I need to holla at you real quick," I said to her.

“I know your thoughts, Goon. I’m not up for that discussion,” she spat with her eyes turning gold.

“Oh, word?” I asked, walking towards her.

“I’m tired and I just want to sleep. I’m stuffed,” she said, rubbing her stomach.

“You are not supposed to hunt alone!” I barked at her.

“I can handle myself,” she said rolling her eyes at me. My canines grew out of my gums, and my breathing sped up. “Do you want to challenge me?” I asked her.

I reached out to touch her, and she scratched my face in retaliation. It was that tattoo she had gotten that was doing this to her; she couldn’t control it. My cheek closed up from the deep wounds on my face that she gave me. Kanya covered her mouth with tears in her eyes. “Baby, I’m so sorry. What’s happening to me?” she asked sadly.

“You are becoming me, your rage, your strength, and not being able to control your beast,” I said to her.“You have to control it, Kanya.”

“Shut the fuck up, Goon! I’m sick of all your bickering and go tend to our twins,” she said, getting into our bed.

“What the fuck did you just say to me?” I asked her.

"I'm tired, and all you are doing is nagging me," she yawned. I charged into Kanya sinking my teeth into her neck. I wasn't trying to kill her; I was showing her that I am the aggressive one. It was a love bite. It was to show her that I am her Alpha. She tried fighting me off.

"You may be a part of me, but your strength will never be stronger than mine. I am Akua, your Alpha, and you will treat me as such," I spoke into her head. Her nails sharpened and pierced through my skin like needles. I growled, biting her harder as she whimpered in pain. Her arousal filled the air, and a howl escaped from my throat. Kanya stopped trying to fight me. She started moaning. My hand slipped between her legs; she was wet.

"*Goon, please enter me,"* her voice whined into my head. I pulled away from her as she tore my sweat pants into shreds. She tore my t-shirt off me. She pulled me down onto the bed, and gently bit my neck. My dick hardened; it needed to find its way inside of her. I rolled her over, propping her ass up into the air. I spread her cheeks gently as my nose nuzzled inside of her. I missed her arousal. She whimpered. I slowly licked between her wet folds, and she arched her back more. I palmed each cheek as my tongue gave her pleasure. I pulled her bud into my mouth, sucking gently on it. My teeth gently bit into her pussy lips. Kanya had an orgasm causing her body to tremble. I didn't want to do this, but I had to tame her. I am the leader of my pack. I have to show that I can lead them. I cannot have my mate challenging me in front of my pack—that's disrespect.

After I licked her dry, I sat up on the bed. Kanya had sweat beads rolling down her tatted back from the pleasure she just received. I gripped the back of her neck with my sharp nails, digging into her skin. She couldn't move. I gently slid inside of her, making myself grow a little more. I stretched her open, and her body tensed up.

"SSSHHHHHHHHHHHHH! It's too big. It's too much," she whined. I ignored her then slowly pulled out of her. I gripped the back of her neck tighter then thrust all of me inside of her. I gave Kanya every single inch of me. She let out a hoarse cry. Gold hairs pierced through her skin. Her mane grew longer with the tips turning brownish-gold. Her nails shredded the sheets as I pumped into her. She tightened her muscles around me to keep me from going deeper. I leaned forward then bit her shoulder, making her loosen up—she was wetter. Her scent started to fill up the room. Every thrust I gave her caused her to howl out. I was too big for her, but her beast wanted me to fuck her. Her beast was getting wetter for me. I pulled out of her then slowly slid back in.

"I'm cummmmiinnnggggggggggggg!" she howled out followed with a growl. I pushed her face further into the mattress as I went harder.

"Talk shit now, Kanya. I don't hear that shit! You sounding like a little puppy over there," I teased going harder and faster, causing the head board to slam into the wall. The wall directly behind the headboard began to form a crack that traveled all the way up to the ceiling. Pieces of paint fell on us, but I didn't stop. A howl escaped my throat when her pussy squeezed me tightly almost causing me to fall forward.

"GGRRRRRRRRRRRRRRRR!" I said loudly. My dick swelled up as I was on the verge of busting. The sounds of her ass cheeks slapping against me filled the room. I sped up until I emptied myself inside of her. I collapsed on top of her, her sweaty hair stuck to my face. After a few seconds, I pulled myself out of Kanya. I rolled her over, and she was still breathing fast. I laughed at her.

"I love you, Kanya," I said kissing her face. She growled at me, causing me to laugh even harder.

"You are lucky; I'm not in the mood," she smirked.

I ran her bath water, adding her favorite oils inside of the tub. I pulled her into me when I joined her inside of the tub. "I miss this," she said kissing my lips.

"I had to bite the hell out of you just to remind you who I am," I said, moving her thick, kinky hair out of her face.

"That seriously hurt. I even stopped breathing for a few seconds. I felt like I was being suffocated."

"I had to show you who was Alpha in this pack," I said, washing her back.

After Kanya got out of the tub, I took a shower then got dressed. Kanya sat up in bed nursing the twins. "So, you are going out with Izra?" she asked me.

"Yeah, I am. I don't want to hear no shit about it neither," I said, kissing her forehead then the twins. Kanya rolled her eyes at me. I chuckled then walked out of our bedroom. When I got outside, Izra was sitting in his Camaro smoking a blunt. When I got inside of the car, he passed it to me.

"You are my nigga. I heard Kanya up there sounding like a newborn puppy. But, nigga, when you howled I was like that's my fucking brother," Izra said, patting my back.

"Yo, seriously? You would be the only dumb muthafucka' to listen to us. Where are we going?" I asked him, reclining the seat back.

"We going to the club, my nigga, V.I.P and all."

"I been telling you since this slang "nigga" came up to stop calling me that shit," I said to Izra, blowing the smoke out of my mouth.

"Nigga, seriously? Let the slavery days go. This is the new world that we live in, and I fucking love it. The style, the clothes, the bitches, the music. I love all of it, and you love it too, so stop fronting. You going to be like Amadi and Elle scared of this new generation," Izra said.

I chuckled. "It is refreshing though, but that nigga shit is for the birds," I told Izra. If it wasn't for Izra and me always going out, we would've been behind with the new generation. We adapted faster than anyone else.

*****

We sat in our section sipping Henny. Izra was lighting up his blunt. "I miss Adika already," he blurted out.

"You got me out here to talk about a damn witch?"

"Seriously, I miss her. I almost can't think without her."

"That's because you marked her," I said to him. A strange scent was in the air. I sniffed. The scent was familiar, but I couldn't point it out.

"You smell that?" I asked Izra.

"Another wolf," Izra said.

When I turned around, it was Dash and a few other guys. Dash was the new Alpha of Xavier's pack. His pack wasn't strongly bonded like mines. Xavier's old pack was made up of wolves from all over the world. Any lone wolf could join his pack. My pack was from ancestry. Amadi's,

Izra's, Elle's and Dayo's parents all served my parents ages ago. They were peasants who worshipped the wolf god in return to get the chance to live for eternity by becoming immortals.

"Look what we have here. Isn't it the Egyptian prince?" one wolf asked and the others laughed.

I chuckled. "In the flesh but what's up? Is there an issue that needs to be taken outside?" I asked the dark-skinned guy that was standing next to Dash. The other wolf standing with them growled at me.

Dash smirked. "Be easy, fellas. We have to worship this nigga," Dash spat angrily.

Izra stood up. "Y'all muthafuckas haven't learned yet? How many pack brothers have y'all lost in these past few months when Xavier was here? Do y'all not know what the fuck is up with us?" Izra growled.

"You let him speak for you, Goon? But I'm not surprised that he doesn't have any manners. He did piss on our tree on our territory, and it stinks. That alone is pack violation," Dash spoke.

I chuckled. “What is supposed to happen? Let’s be clear, Dash, if what he did was an issue, you should’ve challenged him at that moment. Like I stated before, if there is an issue let me know. I’m up for a fight. I hate to say this, but Xavier’s punk ass kept me entertained. Now that he’s gone, I’m assuming you are next runner-up. Don’t worry. I’ll try not to bite you too hard. Your neck looks a little frail,” I said, calmly sipping my Henny. Izra roared in laughter. Dash’s eyes turned yellow; his beast wanted to attack me. “I guess this conversation is over,” I said, bopping my head to the music. Dash and his pack brothers walked off. I turned to Izra and chuckled.

“So, you do say nigga in your head? I knew that shit was a front,” Izra laughed. I always forget how well Izra can sometimes listen to all of my thoughts.

“It was on the spur of the moment,” I laughed. A few girls walked passed us giggling. Izra started sniffing the air while I shook my head at him. “You see the one with the short-cut? Her scent is alluring. The scent of the one with the blonde, fake hair isn’t. The one with the blonde hair smells like that shit Kanya be eating,” Izra said.

"I'm a mated man. I'm not allowed to smell another woman's scent," I told him.

"Nigga, just sniff her out. You know what Kanya eats. I can't think of the name."

"Her scent smells like shrimps," I said.

"That's it!" Izra shouted. The two girls walked over to our section. The one with the blonde hair sat down next to Izra. They were both attractive in the face. Their skin was the color of Egyptian sand. The one with the short hair sat down next to me, and Izra was right—her scent was alluring.

"Hi, handsome," she said.

This man is borderline gorgeous. Those tattoos are such a turn on. I wouldn't mind letting him have his way with me. He smells so good. Oh my god! His body is tall and muscular. Thank god he isn't bulky. I hate bulky men, she ranted off in her head.

The short-hair one scooted closer to me. "My name is Sinea. What's your name?" she asked me.

"Goon," I stated. I looked over at Izra, and he wasn't too pleased with the blonde woman sitting on his lap.

I have to throw my True Religion jeans away. She has a nice ass though. Maybe I can plug my nose then fuck her. I want to know if she uses Summer's Eve, like Adika. Damn it! I'm still thinking about her. She must have put a curse on me. That's what she did. Izra ain't never hung up on a woman. I wonder if Amadi has a fragrance for this woman. I bet he does. Maybe I should call him to ask him. All this ass cannot go to waste, Izra thought.

"So, what's going on? Would you like to dance?" Sinea asked me, grabbing my dick. Her eyes widened. "Oh, my heavens," she stated when I pushed her hand away.

"Look who is having fun." I heard a voice coming from behind me. When I turned around, Kanya and Adika were grilling me. Izra pushed the blonde woman off of his lap. "Ouch, you ass hole!" the woman screamed at Izra.

Kanya had on a pair of tight jeans and a tan leather jacket that was unzipped, showing her cleavage. On her feet were a pair of pumps. I don't know how it's possible, but every time I see her, my stomach drops. I was infatuated with my mate. She is drop-dead gorgeous. Her slanted eyes pierced through me.

"You hear that? It sounds like a dog is in the club. Where is that growling coming from?" Sinea asked, unaware of the dirty looks Kanya was giving her. Kanya's beast wanted to come out, but she was fighting it. Kanya knows that we cannot shift around humans. Our world is separate from the human world, even if we live in it.

"Elle has the twins?" I asked Kanya.

"I just knew this nigga had a baby mama. He's too damn fine. I just knew it was a catch to something," Sinea said, getting up.

"Oh no, sweetie, I'm his wife," Kanya said sitting down next to me.

"Well, he didn't tell me that!" Sinea shouted as she stood up.

"Did you give him a chance to?" Sinea rolled her eyes then walked off. The blonde one took her drink then threw it on Izra. "That's for pushing me onto the floor you jerk." When she walked past Adika, her blonde wig flew up into the air then disappeared.

"My hair!" she screamed, running through the crowd.

"That's my—" Izra got out before Adika cut him off.

"Go ahead and say bitch," Adika warned him.

"I was going to say witch, damn," Izra smirked.

Kanya crossed her arms, giving me an evil look.

"What?" I asked.

"I ought to bite the hell out of you. You left me home with the twins for this?" she yelled at me.

"I'm just chilling, and I didn't leave you home. Besides, that's where you're supposed to be. I tried to give you your privacy. What, I got to be up in your head a lot again?" I asked her.

She mushed my head back. "Don't play with me. Don't you do it. Did she make you aroused?" Kanya asked me.

"Where is this coming from?" I asked her.

"Nigga, do I need to keep reminding you that Kanya is from the new generation? She has that black woman, 'I don't take shit from a nigga' attitude. Your old ass needs to get hipped," Izra said as Adika pinched him.

"No, I didn't get aroused. What are you accusing me of?" I asked Kanya.

"Cheating, nigga!" Izra said.

"Let them talk. Let's dance, and while we're at it, you can explain why you wanted Amadi's oil. I read your thoughts, and it hasn't even been two days since we broke up. I didn't even break up with you. I just said I needed to think about us, and now you're planning to screw someone?" Adika yelled at Izra.

"Here we go with this bullshit," Izra said, standing up. Adika put her hands on her hips, looking up at Izra. "Why are you looking at me like that? You miss the dick don't you? Go ahead and touch it. I promise I will behave," Izra said.

"This is what I'm talking about! That's all you care about; our relationship is built on sex!" Adika screamed making the glasses on the table burst, including the glass I had in my hand.

"I'm out, Kanya. Call me when you get home." Adika then stormed off with Izra following behind her trying to apologize.

"I guess it's just us. I don't mind though. We can use this alone time," I said, waving the waitress over.

“Do you have thoughts about other women?” Kanya asked me.

“No, I don’t. You can hear my thoughts anytime you want to, so I don’t understand why you are asking me that. Can we not fuss though? We are going to turn our beasts against each other. I don’t want that to happen because neither one of us can control our beasts, especially you.”

“You look handsome, by the way. I forgot to tell you that.” Kanya sipped from the wine glass the waitress just gave her. I scooted closer to her then put my arm around her. “What do you want to do about that?” I asked, gently biting her ear. Kanya blushed as my hand rubbed her thigh. “Stop it,” she whined. I invaded her mind…

Kanya was walking through the woods with a red hooded cape on. Her kinky tendrils were falling down her face. She was carrying a brown basket. My icy blue eyes stared at her, and then a growl escaped my throat.

“Who is there?” she called out. I didn’t answer her. She continued to walk deeper into the woods. I followed behind her, my wolf blending in with the night. My husky

paw stepped on a tree branch, causing it to snap. Kanya dropped the basket then turned around with her golden eyes.

I slowly walked towards her with my canines showing. She open up her cape. She was naked underneath. "I just want to go and visit my grandmother, Goon," she said, pretending to be Little Red Riding Hood. I shifted into human form then captured her lips. She backed up against the tree then wrapped her leg around me. I gently bit her lip. Kanya reached down between my legs to grab my hardened dick while I lifted her other leg up. I held her up as she put me into her. She was dripping on the damp ground.

"UMMMMMMMMMMM," she moaned when I pushed a little more of myself into her. I captured her round nipple into my mouth. She let out a howl as I slowly thrust myself into her, her sharpened nails digging into my shoulders. "I love you so much," she cried out in pleasure. I went further inside of her tunnel making deep, hard thrusts that caused her to scream out my name. Her pussy

squeezed me; she was ready to climax. I bit her breast giving her that euphoric orgasm that she craves…

When we came to, the music was still playing loudly in the club. Kanya's head was leaning back over my arm. Her legs were spread, and her chest heaved up and down. "I cannot believe you just mind fucked me. It felt so real. I had an orgasm," she said, fanning herself. I licked her lips. "You want the real thing?" I asked, placing her hand on my hardened dick.

"Are you a witch?" she asked me.

"My mother is."

"That makes you a witch too."

"Males aren't witches. We are warlocks but I prefer my beast," I said chuckling. I figured out what I was when I learned that my mother was a witch, but my beast is more aggressive.

"This is still like a dream," she said.

"I know, but it's what we are."

"Why did I have to be Little Red Riding Hood?"

"I don't know. I thought it was sexy," I laughed.

“I was hoping to be Belle.”

“Who is that?”

“She was a character in Beauty and the Beast. It’s funny because that was my favorite Disney movie. Now, I have my real beast. The only difference is that I’m one too.”

Keora

I walked down to the dungeon underneath my house. Dayo was leaning against the wall as he sat on the floor. I could see it in his eyes that he was giving up fighting.

"I'm home," I called out to him.

"Great," he said, standing up. His strong back muscles flexed. Dayo was tall and lean. His skin was the color of midnight, and he had a pair of hazel eyes. The hair on his face grew out. Even though he hadn't shaved, he was strikingly handsome.

"I brought you some water," I said, pushing the pitcher towards his cell. The iron gate had a spell cast on it. Even if Dayo gets too close without touching it, it shocks him, making him weak. Nobody can detect him, not even the gods. It took me thousands of years to master my spells, but I had to make a sacrifice. I sacrificed my soul to a demon named Saka. My soul was too pure to practice black magic.

I haven't been pure in centuries. I have become a better witch since then. Naobi is pure, and not even she can detach demonic spells, another reason why I chose to sacrifice my soul.

"I don't want any fucking water. I want to go the fuck home. What are you gaining by this? Goon is still with his mate, and you are still here being an evil bitch!" his deep voice boomed.

"Oh, trust me, darling. Being a perfectionist takes time," I answered him. I put three big bloody steaks through the cage. I needed Dayo to be alive because once he dies, I can no longer transform into him. I can't transform into the dead…yet.

"I hope you fucking die a slow and horrible death," he said to me.

"That's not the way to talk to your mate," I laughed. Dayo is the real wolf that marked me. I told Goon that he marked me when he really didn't. I wanted to see how much he remembered, and just like I knew, he didn't remember us at all. I seduced Dayo months back. The sex was so intense I made him bite me. In order for me to shift into his wolf, I needed to be marked by one. I wasn't an animal shifter like Adika, which was the only choice I was left with.

"You tricked me! You hypnotized me into biting you. I would've never marked a piece of ass like you," Dayo seethed.

"Dayo, please don't make me angry."

"I'm fucking trapped in a cage! Do you think I care about your crazy, ancient, old, evil ass being mad? Do it look like I fucking care?" Dayo shouted, charging into the cage. The cage burned him, and he fell back grabbing his arm. "Ow, fuck!" he screamed out in pain.

I laughed. "You will remain here until I'm done with you."

A maniacal laugh came out of Dayo. "You are going to die before me."

"I've been around for years—thousands, might I add. I don't give a damn about dying," I said to him. Dayo turned his back towards me. He had a few tribal markings but not the same as Goon's. Dayo had the markings of a warrior like the other pack brothers in Goon's pack. His nicely muscled legs looked like they could leap over the highest fence. As I looked at him, something started to throb between my legs. I hated the cravings I had for Dayo. I shouldn't have let him mark me, but I was desperate. Now, I sexually crave him, and he craves me too, but he hates me. I appeared in the cage. Dayo tried to charge into me, but I used a force to restrain him. He couldn't move.

"What are you doing to me?" he asked.

"You already know what I want," I said to him, grabbing him; he grew in my hands. I looked him in the face. His eyes were lighter. Dayo wanted to shift but he couldn't. The dungeon was cursed, and it stripped him of his powers. He tried to move but he couldn't.

"Get the fuck off of me," he spat.

"Why would I do such a thing? You belong to me." I lifted my leg up, wrapping it around his waist. I balanced myself by wrapping my other leg around his waist. Dayo couldn't hold me up. I hugged him around his neck with my legs tightly wrapped around him. I raised myself up then lowered myself onto his shaft. Dayo tried to bite me, but I moved out of the way. He was paralyzed while standing up. Dayo's length and width filled me; he was hard and strong. I grinded my hips on him as I kissed his neck, avoiding his mouth. A moan slipped from his mouth as I slid up and down on him.

"This is wrong," he moaned. Dayo got harder, and a pain surged through my lower back, but I couldn't stop moving. I went faster and harder. Dayo's dick jerked when I screamed out in pleasure from my orgasm. After I was done, I unwrapped my wobbly legs. I began to rub his chest, and I had an urge to kiss him.

What is wrong with me? I asked myself. I hurriedly disappeared. I ended up on the other side of the cage. Dayo's body fell down on the stone floor. He sat up then looked at me with the most intense stare. I could see the pure hate he had for me in his eyes. I looked away then headed upstairs. I slid the door open. When I got into my living room, I shut the door that looked like a wall from the outside. I slid my bookshelf in front of it. I was glad that it was sound proof. I heard a noise coming from the kitchen. I wrapped my silk robe tightly around my body. "Do you not call when you come over?" I asked Adika.

Adika turned around. “Since when do I have to call? You know I been meaning to talk to you. You’ve been acting weird. You block me from your mind, and I just feel like I don’t know you anymore. Do you want to talk about it?” she asked me.

I rolled my eyes at her. “What is there to talk about?”

“The freaking attitude, Keora! I’m sick of it!”

“Well, stop dropping by whenever you feel like it.”

“It’s Goon isn’t it? Get the fuck over it! You haven’t been with him in years! I mean, how do you even know what he still feels like?” Adika asked me.

“You mean to tell me you feel nothing for Kofi still? Before he mated, weren’t you fucking him? Does Izra know that you use to bang his mentor? I remember how much you two was in love, and now he acts like he doesn’t remember you. How does that feel?”

“That was thousands of years ago. I got over him. I cannot even remember what Kofi feels like. Your ass is just evil. Evil cannot let anything go. Naobi didn’t create us to be this way,” Adika said. I rolled my eyes because she still worships Naobi like she did when we were in Egypt.

"You act just like a peasant. They brainwashed you. Naobi and Ammon are just two ancient muthafuckas that control every damn body that lived in Egypt all of those years ago. Fuck Naobi and Ammon," I said with my hair growing. I wanted to strangle Adika until she took her last breath. I hated her. If Adika ever died, so would I. That's the only reason why I have been tolerating her.

"Have you been practicing black magic?" Adika asked me.

"Excuse me?"

"Your eyes just turned pitch black. I've only seen one person with black eyes ages ago, and that was Saka. I will never forget him. I will never forget those demon eyes, and you have eyes just like his. What have you been doing? Did you get in touch with him? Naobi sent him to a dark world, and he is never supposed to come back. What did you do, Keora?" Adika asked me.

I laughed. "I don't know what you are talking about," I said, walking away. Adika yanked my locks back. "Bitch, I would beat your ass! What the fuck did you do? Saka is forbidden. Remember how he wanted Goon when he was a baby? He wanted Goon's soul. You was there! You saw what he did to the people; he turned them into blood sucking monsters. You brought him back?" Adika screamed.

I flipped her off of me then banged her head into the counter. Her wound closed up. Adika turned into a panther then attacked me. She bit my neck with her teeth, piercing into my neck.

Remember, sister, if you kill me, you will die with me too. Now, you can tell Naobi, and you will go to the underworld with me. I know you wouldn't want that. What would Izra do? I said into her head. She let me go.

Adika shifted back. "What did you do?" she asked with tears falling down her face. I smiled at her. "Get the fuck out of my house."

"Saka is a demon. He gets powerful off of innocent, pure blood. You sacrificed yourself in return of the twins. What have you done?" Adika cried.

"Those twins should've been mine," I said to Adika. Adika ranted on as I thought of ways to get rid of her without killing her. An idea formed inside of my head. I walked to the hidden wall then pushed the bookshelf back.

"I'm sorry. I have done a bad thing. Maybe you can help me get Dayo out," I said, pushing the wall back.

"WHAT?" she asked.

"I have done a terrible thing, Adika. Maybe you can help me get Dayo out. I walked down the cold stone steps towards Dayo's cage. "What the hell is this? You did this? You been pretending to be him?" Adika asked. The cage opened up. Dayo looked up with worried eyes. Adika walked into the cage. "Get the hell out. It's a trapped!" Dayo tried to warn Adika, but the cage slammed shut. Adika ran into the bars of the cage, but then let out a scream because it burned her skin.

"Adika, darling. You have been trying to be so much of a human that you even think stupidly like one. Did you really think that I was going to let you leave out of this damn house? See what I mean about having a pure heart? You think too much of others without seeing the bigger picture. You and I would be untouchable if you gave up your pureness. Your heart is too good, and that will fuck you over in the long run," I said to her.

"Get us out!" Adika screamed.

"Stop wasting your breath. Just know this dungeon strips you from everything. You won't even be able to shift. See, Dayo, I'm not bad after all. I gave you someone to play with," I said laughing.

Adika backed away from the cage with a smirk on her face. "Kanya is going to beat your ass, and the only thing I'm pissed about is that I won't be able to be there to cheer her on."

"You know, I always wanted to know what it felt like to walk a mile in your shoes. Maybe Kanya and I can be best friends, or maybe I can fuck Izra. Oh wait, I can get to the twins," I smiled, realizing that I should've been using Adika all along.

"Stay the fuck away from Izra." Adika screamed.

"Awww, you love him? How sweet. All the merrier," I said, walking out of the dungeon.

I went upstairs into my room where I practiced all of my spells. I pushed a few ancient books off my desk, and then transformed into Dayo because I needed his handwriting. I wrote the pack a letter saying his good-bye. I was getting nowhere as Dayo. I could start over with my plan. I had to hurry because Naobi doesn't stay out of the loop too long, and I didn't need the distraction.

"You are not the only powerful bitch," I spat loudly as if Naobi could hear me.

Kanya

"Where are you taking me? And why do you have me blocked from your mind?" I asked Goon.

"Have I ever told you how nosey you are? It's a surprise. Now sit back and wait for it," he spat, getting annoyed.

"I don't like surprises," I laughed.

"Me neither. If I knew you would be this annoying about it, I wouldn't be trying to surprise you," he chuckled.

I rode in the passenger seat with a pair of blindfolds on. We have been driving for quite some time. Well, I thought it was a long time, but the truth was I just really wanted to know what Goon had in store for me. He has been really busy this past week; he has also been blocking me from his thoughts a lot. He was up to something, and I couldn't wait to find out.

The truck came to a stop. Goon opened up the door, pulling me out. He grabbed my hand and wrapped his other arm around my hip to keep me from falling as we started walking.

"Is this some type of freaky foreplay?" I asked Goon.

"If you want it to be. I'm addicted to your pussy," he said. I heard the sounds of keys jingling. Moments later, my heels were clicking on what sounded like marble floors.

"Okay, take the blindfolds off," Goon said to me. I hurriedly took them off. I was standing in a large building with pretty white marble floors. There were a few chandeliers hanging from the high ceilings. There were empty showcase glasses displayed all around the large area. I was confused.

"This is a very nice place, but help me understand," I said, looking up into his handsome face.

"This is your jewelry store. You always said you wanted to own your own business. I have been feeling guilty about the way you had to adapt to being my mate. I want you to still feel normal."

Words couldn't explain how much I loved him. The love was so strong that it felt like I had loved him for years. In just a short amount of time, I met my soul mate and gave him pups. At times I felt like I was stuck in a dream; I felt like I was living in some fairy tale. I was a beast. I was Goon's beast, and I didn't want it any other way. When I first found out who I really was, I couldn't accept it, but now I wouldn't have it any other way.

"I fall in love with your more and more every day. This is so beautiful," I said, still surprised.

Goon kissed my lips. "I know you do because I feel the same way. How you feel now is how I felt when you birthed my pups. It was beautiful, although the sight of you giving birth made my stomach turn," he said.

I playfully mushed him. "You just had to ruin my moment," I said. I looked around the spacious store. It looked upscale, almost too rich.

"Goon, what kind of jewelry will I be selling here? This place almost looks like an art museum."

He smirked. "Egyptian jewelry, real gold and gems. We have a lot of it locked away. They are worth a lot of money in this day and age. We also have jewelry from other places we have traveled to over the centuries. Let me worry about everything."

Would I embarrass myself if I broke out into doing the cabbage patch, I thought to myself. Then Goon laughed.

"Nobody does that anymore. All the women do a dance called twerking now," Goon said surprisingly.

"How do you know about that?"

"I know everything. I'm old in years, but I'm still young," he laughed.

Goon locked up the store. On the outside, my store looked like a warehouse. I loved it. It was one of those buildings that will have you curious about what's on the inside. On our way home, I was thinking about what to name my store.

"I want Amadi to sell some of his oils in the store. I want him to have his own section. This will be great! I can see it now," I said excitedly.

"Amadi doesn't really like to be around humans much. Every once in a while he would come out with Izra and I. I will let you talk to him about that," Goon said.

"What do you think we should name the store?" I asked Goon as he punched in the code on the gate to the mansion.

"Beastly Treasures, that's what I nicknamed your pussy," he roared into laughter.

"Even though you are being an asshole right now,I actually like that," I said, rolling my eyes. When we walked into the house, Elle came down the stairs looking exhausted, holding the twins in his arms.

"Thank the gods you two are back. These pups are a handful. Remind me to beg the gods to take me into their world when the twins start shifting," Elle said, giving me my babies.

"My babies aren't a handful," I said growling.

"Bro, please don't piss her off. Her beast has been on good behavior." Goon warned Elle; then they started laughing. I headed towards the kitchen. It was hard at times living with cocky men who were beasts. The doorbell rang. "Goon, get the door. It's Adika!" I shouted out.

Adika texted me minutes before I came home to tell me that she was coming over for dinner. She and Izra were still on their fall out. Adika walked into the kitchen humming. "Wow, you are happy today. Did you and Izra make up?" I asked her.

"No, we didn't. I actually met someone else."

"Come again?" I said to her. She reached out for Akea, and he started crying. "That's weird. He usually likes when you hold him," I said looking at her. Goon walked into the kitchen.

"What's wrong with him?" Goon asked.

"I don't know. I can't feel what's wrong with him yet. It bothers me that I still can't feel their feelings." Goon took Akea away from Adika, and then walked back out of the kitchen.

"He is a very protective father. I always wanted a family," she said.

"It will come; you just have to be patient. Izra would be a good father. I can see him now."

"Izra is still a young wolf. He can't get me pregnant any time soon. He hasn't reached that peek yet."

"So, he's shooting blanks?" I asked her.

"Yup, until it's his time to mate."

Amadi came into the kitchen. "Izra has reached his peek. That's why he bit you. When a male wolf has an urge to bite his mate, that means he is marking her to get her pregnant when its time," Amadi butted in.

"WHAT!" Adika screamed.

"Izra marked you so when his time comes, you will give him pups," Amadi said.

"I shouldn't had screwed that bastard," Adika mumbled. Izra must have pissed Adika off because she always wanted a family. She sounded as if she regretted Izra.

Izra came into the house with his motorcycle gear on and walked past Adika. He took a pitcher of water out of the fridge then guzzled it down.

He sniffed the air. "I guess this is one of your spells, huh? Change your scent so I won't bother you. I really made you that mad?" Izra asked her.

"Don't flatter yourself punk," Adika spat.

"Bitch," Izra spat, walking out of the kitchen.

I gave Kanye to Amadi so Goon could bathe him while Adika and I chatted.

"Goon bought me a store," I said cheerfully.

"Oh really?" she asked with a hint of sarcasm in her voice.

"Why are you acting like a bitch? You been acting weird since you came in. You disrespected Izra, and now you are trying to disrespect me," I said to her. My beast wanted to attack her. I felt a ball of rage build up inside of me. I could feel my body trying to shift. Lately, I have been having these angry spells. The slightest thing ticked me off. Adika smirked at me. "Oh, don't mind me. I'm just in a funk. Continue on," she said, waving me off.

"What's bothering you?" I asked her.

"Nothing, I'm cool."

"Who is this new man?"

"Oh, nobody. Just someone I screw whenever I want. He is my little secret," she laughed.

Elle walked into the kitchen reading a piece of paper; he must have just checked the mail.

“What’s that?” I asked Elle.

“A letter from Dayo. He’s left the pack. He feels like you have ruined it, and he wants no part of it. We been a pack for one hundred-plus years, and we never been apart. We are built in tradition. I don’t know what to do,” Elle said sadly.

“Well, he was isolated anyway. I barely saw him when I came over, so it was only a matter of time,” Adika said.

“This doesn’t concern you. You are not a part of this pack, so don’t speak on it. We have some things to discuss within this pack, so get the fuck out!” Elle roared. I have never seen Elle upset. He was like the uncle of the pack. Adika grabbed her purse then stormed out of the house.

“That was rude,” I said to Elle.

“I don’t give a damn, Kanya. This is a serious matter. You don’t know what it’s like for a wolf to be a loner. There is another pack in this town. If they get wind of Dayo, he is doomed,” Elle said. Goon, Amadi, and Izra came downstairs. They all had a bond; they knew when one of the pack was upset.

"What's going on?" Amadi asked Elle. Elle handed Amadi the letter from Dayo.

"He left because of Kanya?" Amadi asked. I started to feel guilty because I broke up something that they had for years. Tears welled up in my eyes. "I didn't mean to do it," I said.

"Maybe you should've made him more comfortable," Elle said to me.

"Speak to me, Elle, when I'm in my mate's presence. You know the rules," Goon said to Elle.

"I get that she is your mate, but shit wasn't supposed to be like this. It's almost like Kanya is a curse. Two pack brothers are now gone," Elle said to Goon.

"Come on, bro. You can't blame this shit on Kanya. It was time for Kofi to go back to his world, and it's not her fault Dayo wanted some wolf dick and couldn't get it," Izra said. Before I knew it, Elle was in wolf form attacking Izra, who had immediately shifted. I backed away because when wolves fight, it gets ugly.

Elle's wolf was bigger than Izra's because Izra was still a young wolf, but Izra was more of a fighter. Elle's wolf was gray, brown and white. Elle sank his teeth into Izra's stomach. Izra let out a howl. They both were rolling around breaking up furniture. Amadi hollered for them to stop. Blood splattered on the wall when Izra bit Elle's neck. Goon's wolf started to pull them apart. Everything happened so fast that I didn't realize Goon had shifted. Somehow all three of them ended up in the living room. Three huge animals were rolling around breaking up everything in sight. Izra accidentally bit Goon. Elle charged into Izra, with Goon still in the middle. All three of them went through the wall, landing in their gym room.

"Do something, Amadi!" I screamed.

Amadi ran down the hall then came back with a whistle. When he blew it, Goon, Elle and Izra immediately shifted back into human form.

I turned my head to ignore looking at Elle and Izra, who were both naked and bloody. Even though I have saw them naked plenty of times, I was forbidden from looking at them.

Goon looked at Amadi with blue eyes. His fangs were hanging out of his mouth. "I hate that damn whistle," Goon roared. Goon looked like he wanted to attack Amadi.

"It was the only way," Amadi said.

"Kofi should've taken that shit with him," Izra said. Elle growled at Izra.

"Cut it out! This is our little brother. You had no business attacking him," Goon said, shoving Elle into the wall.

"Fuck him! He always talks shit not remembering he can get his little ass kicked! He needs to show respect for all of his brothers, despite what he thinks of them. Even if Dayo likes men, it doesn't give Izra no damn right to judge him. Dayo has saved Izra from a lot of shit in the past. Perhaps Izra has forgotten about that because all he wants to do is live like a human and speak ridiculous slang," Elle fussed.

"Oh, shut the fuck up, nigga! That's your problem, Elle. You are still trying to live isolated from the world. Nigga, this is what we live in; we live in society with humans. Get your mind out of the damn woods and accept that we are going to live like humans," Izra spat.

"We need to stick together!" Amadi shouted.

"No one fights inside of the house. If you want to rip each other's throats apart, take it to the woods," Goon said.

"Shut the fuck up, nigga. You was just ripping Dayo apart a few months ago at the dining room table. My damn orange juice spilled on the floor because of that shit," Izra said.

I went upstairs to our bedroom. The twins were in their cribs sleeping peacefully while the pack was still arguing, and I heard growling and a few more things breaking. I guess a fight broke out again. It pained me to watch them fight. It made me nervous because when they were in beast mode, they didn't care about one another.

Moments later, Goon came into our bedroom. He flopped down on the bed completely naked.

"I had to give Amadi some of my blood. Elle and Izra attacked each other again. Amadi tried to pull them apart in human form and got attacked by them. Amadi knows that you cannot pull beasts apart in human form," Goon said.

"Why did they fight again?"

"Elle broke Izra's PlayStation," Goon said.

My mother texted me telling me she wanted to see the babies; she wanted our address. I send them pictures of the twins daily, but truth is I'm afraid to tell them what I am.

The next morning, I got up early to hire some staff for my store. The night before, while everyone was asleep, I surfed the internet all night posting hiring ads on job sites. Three people responded immediately. I was going to meet them at the store. On my way out of the door, Elle, Amadi and Izra were laughing at each other while cleaning up.

"Good-morning, Kanya. I apologize for my rudeness yesterday," Elle said.

"It's okay. We all have our moments," I said, still not believing how well they were getting along.

Pack brothers fight all the time then next day it's forgotten, Goon said inside of my head.

I can see that, I answered.

I opened up the door to my store. I was excited. I still couldn't believe Goon did all of this for me. I was walking around getting ideas of how I would decorate my store. A scent of another wolf filled the air, along with sounds of clicking heels.

"Beautiful place," a voice said from behind me. When I turned around, Amilia was staring coldly at me.

"What are you doing here?" I asked her.

"I'm here for the same reason you are," Amilia said to me.

"This is my store, Amilia. Interviews don't start for another twenty minutes." When Amilia and I worked at the club together, we were cordial. But when she tried to attack Goon to defend Xavier, it changed my opinion about her. Amilia's wolf was all white with green-like eyes; her wolf was beautiful.

"The early bird gets the worm," Amilia said, looking around. "How does it feel to be mated with an Egyptian prince who has access to a lot of worthy things? You really got lucky didn't you?"

Amilia was pretty. She was of Latina. She reminded me of Jennifer Lopez. She and the new Alpha of Xavier's pack are mated from what I heard.

"I don't call it being lucky, Amilia. I call it fate."

"How are the pups?" Amilia asked me.

"Excuse me if I'm wrong, but last time I checked, you was the one being interviewed. Keep your questions to yourself, Amilia. My life isn't any of your concern."

"Just making small talk. I apologize for my behavior towards you. I was doing what a mate was supposed to do. I didn't love Xavier, but I had to defend him," she said.

"I can understand. I would kill someone if they tried to harm Goon. But you already know about that," I said, reminding her of the time I had to attack her.

"Look, Kanya. I really need a job; my pack is going broke. When Xavier died, they closed down the clubs that were our main source of income. I forget how to live like a human. Xavier and I wasn't married. Nothing was left to me, so now the pack is living off money we had saved. There are a lot of us, and the money is going to run out soon," Amilia said.

"Dash doesn't know I'm trying to work, but I need a job," she begged.

"We are from different packs. I have to think about this."

"Don't you just hate how they have to make rules for everything? We have to live like their children. They dictate what we can and can't do. Do you not see that? They control us, Kanya."

"It's tradition, Amilia."

"It's control! They control us, and we can't do nothing about it. I bet everything you do has to go through Goon first, and he must approve. It's called control. All I want to do is have a place for my pups. you two weren't the only ones who mated during that full moon. I really need a job, and you are my only hope," Amilia said. I got a piece of paper and wrote down what I had to say to Amilia. I didn't want Goon to know what I was up to because he can hear my thoughts. While I was writing down when Amilia could start working, I was thinking about what the pups were doing.

She took the paper then hugged me. “I won’t tell Dash. This is between you and I,” she said. After she left, another woman walked in. She was drop-dead gorgeous. Her skin was like dark chocolate, and her cheekbones were strong, giving her a look that meant powerful. When she walked, it looked like her feet didn’t touch the floor. She wore a long wrapped dress with her hair wrapped up. The gold jewelry she had on looked to be worth a lot.

“Can I help you?” I asked her. She looked like royalty. I doubt she needed to work.

“I finally get to meet you,” she said.

“Who are you?” I hoped she wasn’t crazy. I would hate to bite her neck and get blood all over the floors.

“You even think like my son,” she said in a deep, weird accent that sounded like it came from another time.

Did she hear my thoughts? I asked myself.

“I’m Akua’s mother. I wanted to see this investment myself. Akua has always been very thoughtful of those he cares about.” She said, walking around with her long dress dragging along the floor.

I couldn't speak or look Naobi in her face—her presence was that strong.

"Do not fear me, Kanya. I love you the same way I love my son. You are a part of him. You were chosen for a reason," she said, walking close to me.

"I don't know what to say," I told her.

"I'm on borrowed time. When I cast myself out of the Anubi, I was given only a certain amount of time to get back. We are not allowed here on earth for too long; it weakens us."

"What's Anubi?" I asked her.

"It's the world all of the ancient immortals go to. It's almost like heaven, except we don't die to get there. We have to wait years until it's time for us to go. You and Goon will be there centuries from now," she said.

The door opened and in walked an ebony woman with long, pretty locks. She was dressed comfortably in a pair of black slacks, heels, and a black blazer with a white and black pinstriped shirt on underneath. Her make-up was done nicely, and she was shapely, about a size twelve. She had a very unique look to her, almost like she belonged in a painting.

"Hi, I'm Jalesa. We were scheduled for ten o'clock. I know I'm early, but early means on time," she spoke. When I turned around, Naobi was gone. I looked around for her, but there wasn't a trace of her.

Wow, that was weird, I thought to myself.

We will meet again and soon. Naobi's voice came into my head scaring me, causing me to jump. "Are you okay?" Jalesa asked me.

"Yes, I'm fine. I set up an area right over there in the corner. We will get to know each other, and then we will take it from there," I said to her.

"How old are you, if you don't mind me asking? When I saw an ad for a jewelry store, I was thinking of an older woman, perhaps one from a different country," Jalesa said laughing.

"I'm twenty-three, and my husband got this store for me," I beamed.

"That's amazing. You look very happy," she smiled. Jalesa had a sweet personality, and she was a people person. She would make a wonderful floor assistant. After she and I got to know one another, I hired her on the spot. I still needed to figure out what I could use Amilia for. I didn't want anyone to see her. Goon wouldn't be too happy about that since she is from another pack. I needed to hire six more people. I had a long day ahead of me.

Naobi

"You cannot keep going back to that human world. Why are you doing this? Do you know that you can get stuck there for ages?" Ammon asked me.

"Our son might be in danger. I can feel it. I can see the images," I said.

"Akua is a prince who carries on his father's legacy. He is a strong wolf! You cannot fight his battles! Let him be the Alpha he is; let him take care of everything on his own. Stay away from earth, Naobi. This is not up for questioning. I'm telling you to not go back. We can see Akua's life from here along with the pups," Ammon fussed.

"Don't tell me what to do when it comes to Akua. I'm his mother, and he is and will always be my son. I would sacrifice my soul for him," I spat. I walked down the stone hall in the temple we lived in and pushed the door open.

The sound of Egyptian music played while the immortals feasted.

“My queen, is everything okay?” A voice came from behind me. I turned around and it was Jalesa.

“Yes, everything is fine. Remember what we talked about? No one must know what we are doing. I want you to keep an eye out for those witch sisters. I had an image that one of them had a demon heart, but I cannot detect that from here. Earth weakens my strength. Until I find out how to maintain my strength, you will be my ears and my eyes. I want you to protect those pups, and remember the spells I taught you,” I said to Jalesa.

Jalesa bowed her head down. “Yes, my queen,” she said.

“Now, go on my dear,” I said to her, excusing her. Jalesa went off. She was a human servant. I had taken to her ages ago when I lived on earth. Her family was murdered by Saka. I had saved her before he took her innocent soul. Saka fed off of innocence. Jalesa was a servant until she got old and died. With her blood, I reincarnated her. I made her immortal; she will never get old again. I taught her from a little girl about spells and curses; she was like my daughter.

Before Jalesa, I created Adika and Keora. Saka was taking souls to gain his power. A pure witch and wolf blood baby are what Saka needs to be in human form again. Adika and Keora were created to protect Goon from Saka. I cast a spell that put him away for eternity, but someone awakened him. Saka was a warlock, until he realized how taking souls could make his power stronger. In turn, he turned into an evil demon. The evil demon, Saka, was my father. He wanted my son, and now he wants his grandson, Akea. Akea has witch and wolf blood; a very powerful combination. If my images are true, then that means that Saka will have Akea's soul, and he will be able to be in human form again.

Ammon came from behind me with his gold metal cup of wine. "Come on. Let's dance," he said, pulling on me.

"Not now, Ammon," I said to him.

"I want my mate back, Naobi. I want to see your pretty smile. I want to see you dance and feel free," his deep voice said to me. I looked into his handsome face. He didn't look a day over forty. I placed my hand on his strong and massive chest. He squeezed my hand, looking into my eyes. "I won't rest until I know Akua and his pack are alright," I said to him.

"I will be in my sanctuary. Do not disturb me," I said to Ammon, walking away. Kofi walked down the stone hall.

"Smile, my queen," he said cheerfully.

I patted Kofi on his shoulder. "I haven't gotten a chance to welcome you back home. I appreciate all you have done for us. Help yourself to some fruit and wine. Dance the night away. You and your mate have a lot of time to make up," I said to him then smiled.

"Well, in the words of Izra, I been smashing that all night long," he said laughing. Then he got a sad look on his face. "I miss the pack," Kofi said to me.

"You can always go visit; you just can't stay long," I told him.

"That's the problem, Naobi. If I go visit, I wouldn't want to come back. I wanted so badly to come back home, and now I realize that was my home," Kofi said to me. I didn't have a response to that because it was all my fault why he had been away for so long.

When will you come to me? a voice said inside of my head. His voice gave me chills. I longed for him.

Soon, I responded.

Goon

I sat and watched Kanya and Adika chat while putting the pieces of jewelry in the showcases. I couldn't detect anything from Adika's thoughts, but something wasn't right with her.

"Bro, what are you doing starring at Adika like that? You're not thinking about what I think you're thinking about?" Amadi asked me, carrying a box of his oils.

"Don't fuck with me, bro. You know Kanya's ass is nosey. That's all she needs to do is think I have desires for another woman. I'm more afraid of her snappy attitude than her beast. You know the neck rolling and the hands on the hips?" I asked him.

"Yeah, I've seen her do that plenty of times," Amadi laughed. Jalesa walked into the store. I had met her earlier. I was surprised to see Kanya take to her as fast as she did.

Look at that ass. I want to know what she smells like, Amadi thought to himself.

"Go sniff her. I have learned that looks can be deceiving. Before my mate, I ran into very stunning women, but their scents would scare a vulture, and vultures only eat when the corpse smells at its worst," I told Amadi and he chuckled.

"I'm about to introduce myself to her," Amadi said, eyeing Jalesa.

"If her scent is off, you can always make a special soap for her," I said. Amadi responded with a growl.

"My niggas," Izra said, walking into the store. He had a suitcase in his hand that carried some of the jewelry.

"You are late," I said to him.

"I apologize. I saw this woman with the phattest ass. I mean, her ass was so plump, I wanted to bite into it like a thick, bloody raw piece of meat," he said. Amadi shook his head at Izra. "Damn, who is that over there with Kanya?" Izra asked out loud, talking about Jalesa.

"Don't worry about that," Amadi warned Izra. Izra held his hands up. "My bad, bro. You growling and shit," Izra said laughing.

Adika walked over to us, which caused Izra to start growling. I nudged him because I didn't want Jalesa to hear it.

"Would you chill out?" I asked him.

"That bitch rubs me the wrong way," Izra said to me.

"Hey, lover, you don't love me anymore?" Adika asked, throwing her arms around Izra's neck. He grabbed her arms then moved them from around his neck.

"I'm no longer interested," he said. Adika laughed, kissed his lips then walked out of the store.

"That witch must have gotten ahold of some type of voodoo," Izra said. Kanya walked over to us with Jalesa following behind her. Amadi lustfully stared at Jalesa's hips. "Thirsty-ass nigga," Izra said, laughing.

"Izra and Amadi, this is one of my sales women. Her name is Jalesa. Jalesa, these are my brothers-in-law," Kanya introduced them.

"Hello, it's nice to meet you," Jalesa said with her hand out. Izra shook her hand, but Amadi froze.

Shake her hand! I shouted inside of Amadi's head. Amadi took Jalesa's hand then kissed it. "How are you doing today, beautiful?" Amadi asked Jalesa.

Amadi is making me nervous. He is too attractive, Jalesa panicked inside of her head.

Amadi started smiling. "Can I have a few minutes of your time to talk? I was admiring you when you first came in. Your hair is stunning, by the way," he said smoothly. Jalesa blushed shyly then walked to the other side of the store with Amadi following behind her.

Her scent smells better than all of my oils combined, Amadi thought.

"Amadi got game after all," Kanya said.

"He got that shit from me. That nigga stole my lines," Izra fussed.

"The lies you tell, Izra. 'Damn, girl, you got a phat ass' is more so your speed. You need to learn from my baby Goonie and Amadi because your player card has been revoked," Kanya teased Izra.

"Very funny, but bro, did she just call your big mean ass Goonie?" Izra asked me. I shrugged my shoulders as I continued to lay the jewelry down in the showcase.

We worked all day to get the store in order. There were a few things that still needed to be done.

Everyone left except for Kanya and I. "We have our photo shoot tomorrow," Kanya said.

"For what?" I asked her.

"Advertisement. Beastly Treasures is elegant with a little dark side to it, almost like us," she said.

"Knock yourself out, but I'm warning you, do not wake me up just so I can get a picture taken. Now, let's go hunt; I'm starving," I told her.

*****

Kanya and I roamed around deep into the woods. I picked up a scent of a male deer. Kanya growled when she sniffed the air; there was a wolf in the woods on our territory.

There is another wolf in our woods, I said to her.

I can smell him, she replied.

The sound of bushes rustling started, and a loud growl echoed throughout the woods. I smelled blood; the wolf had gotten to our meal. I ran towards the scent of blood in full speed. Down by a small lake, there was a brown and black wolf feasting on a deer. Two more wolves appeared from out of nowhere. Before I could warn Kanya, she was beside me crouching down. Kanya's head was blocking my neck. Alpha females do that to protect their mate from getting their necks bitten. I never taught her that; it was just instinct.

I growled. Six pairs of eyes stared at me with deer blood dripping from their mouths. The brown and black wolf was Dash. I remembered his scent.

What are you doing in my woods? I said inside of Dash's head.

This buck was on our land and ran into yours so that makes it my meal, he replied back. The other two wolves had their fangs showing with their ears pointed back. They were ready to attack me. I pushed Kanya out of the way then charged into Dash, sinking my canines into his neck. Dash bit my shoulder. He was stronger than Xavier and more of a fighter. I stood up on my hind legs, slinging Dash into a tree. The other two wolves were circling Kanya. One of them sniffed behind her tale. Dash charged into me, and the smell of fresh blood traveled throughout the air.

My claws ripped into Dash's fur, cutting him open. Three deep open gashes ran down his side. Dash was going to fight me until he couldn't anymore. He dropped to the ground then howled. The two wolves were still trying to attack Kanya, but she was too fast. She stood and fought the both of them. One of the wolves tried to get to her neck, but she quickly moved, charging into him and pinning him to a tree. The other wolf leaped on her. I charged into him. My teeth pierced through his stomach like knives. I pulled away, yanking a chunk out of his stomach.

Kanya clamped down tightly on the wolf's neck that she was fighting. He tried to bite her, but he couldn't. She pinned him down, tearing into his neck until his head was barely connected to his body. Dash stood up weakly, blood dripping from his side. Dash bowed his head down; he was surrendering because he was injured. Kanya tried to charge into him, but I stopped her.

After a wolf surrenders, we do not attack, I said. Dash limped away, leaving two wolves behind. His pack was like a gang—every wolf was for himself. I would die before I left a pack brother behind to get killed. One wolf was dead. The other wolf lay on the ground then turned to his human form, he was a white man. A chunk of his stomach was missing. He was going to die slowly, bleeding out.

"You sons of bitches," the white man yelled, spitting up blood. Kanya walked over to him. Her strong canines clamped down onto his neck.

That's it beautiful, I cheered her on as she killed him. He was the one that blatantly sniffed her. He disrespected her. It was almost like a man seeing a woman that he doesn't know, and he slaps her on the behind. Kanya walked over to me with her bushy, long tail trailing behind her. Her gold eyes looked into mines as she nuzzled her face into my neck. I bent my head down to lick the blood off of her face.

Let's go home. I know Elle is going crazy with the pups. Kanya's sultry voice came into my head.

When we made it back to the mansion, we hurriedly went into our bedroom to shower. Kanya was quiet as I washed her back. "What's the matter?" I asked her. She turned around looking into my eyes.

"I felt nothing for those wolves I killed, and I don't regret it. If I could, I would do it all over again. What's the matter with me?"

I lifted her head up by her chin then kissed her lips. "You are a part of me; I feel the same way after I kill. It's in our nature, and never regret anything. They challenged us on our territory," I told her.

"The twins are sleep," Kanya said to me, grabbing at my dick. I immediately got aroused. I picked her up, leaning her against the shower wall. She wrapped her legs around me. I lifted her up to ease her down on my length. She growled then hissed. I pulled out of her, entering her again.

"Open up, Kanya," I groaned. I spread her legs out then went sailing in deeply. Kanya let out a loud noise that sounded like a howl. I hurriedly placed my hand over her mouth.

"You are going to wake the pups," I whispered into her ear as I pumped in and out of her. Her walls squeezed me as she got wetter, and her nipples hardened against my chest. I pulled out, leaving the tip in, then went back into her deeper than I was at first. Her legs shook while her eyes rolled to the back of her head. I pumped furiously into her as her breasts bounced with every stroke I gave her. Her nails went into my skin. I growled as my fangs protruded out.

Bite me! Oh god, Goon. Baby, please bite me, Kanya's thoughts begged.

I uncovered her mouth and noticed her fangs were out. I pulled her head back by her hair as I thrust further into her, causing her to yelp out. My dick widened inside of her;

I was about to explode. Kanya's scent poured out of her and ran down my leg. I felt her heart rate speed up. She wrapped her legs tightly around me, taking all of me. I was too big for her, but her pussy took all of me. I slowed up my pace, kissing on her neck. She moaned out. I licked behind her ear then trailed my tongue down her neck and around her sensitive spot. Kanya squirmed and made noises like she was in pain as my length drilled deeply into her. She was waiting for me to bite her. I looked into her face, and tears were falling from her eyes. The pleasure was so intense she couldn't handle it, even though she craved it. I gripped her hair harder. I pulled her head back further then clamped down onto her neck while I sped up my pace, slamming my dick into her spot over and over again with my teeth sinking into her throat. Kanya made a gasp like she was taking her last breath. Her body went limp, but I held her up. She squirted, and then I released my semen inside of her. The shower water was cold, but that was the least of our worries.

*****

The next morning…

"Goon, wake up! The photographer is almost here, and we need to get ready," Kanya screamed at me with the pups in her arms.

"Damn it, Kanya! I told your ass not to wake me up for that stupid shit," I shouted back, rolling over and burying my face into the pillow. Kanya put the twins in their cribs. She then leaped on my back with her teeth sinking into my shoulder.

"AGGHHHHHHHH! FUCK!" I said, hurriedly getting up. Kanya stood at the side of the bed with her arms crossed. Her thick and kinky tendrils were falling in her face. She frowned, her glossed lips pushed out. "Get up, Goon. We can sleep later. We have to get everything in order for the store," she said, pointing her finger into my solid chest.

I pushed her out of my way then walked into the bathroom while Kanya burst into a fit of laughter.

I stood over the toilet releasing myself. “You want me to hold that for you, daddy?” Kanya taunted me.

“Leave me the fuck alone, Kanya,” I growled.

“You are so grumpy in the morning, but wear something edgy. We need that gothic look. Oh, and Izra has a surprise for us,” Kanya ranted on. After I was done releasing myself, I shook it. Kanya was standing in the doorway staring at me.

“Seriously, leave me alone. I told you not to wake me, and you did it anyway. I keep telling you about that type of behavior. Let me sleep in peace. Damn,” I said to Kanya.

“You are not my father. I’m sick of all this crap about how I have to obey this and that. I’m your other half, not your child,” she ranted on.

“I don’t want to hear that shit this early in the morning. The damn sun isn’t even out yet. Who comes to people’s homes this early anyway? I hope they aren’t scared of animals. I’m walking right into the picture in my big black beast form. I bet that would scare the fuck out of them,” I fussed.

“Asshole,” Kanya said, walking away.

“I’m going to be a bigger one when they get here,” I yelled out behind her, and then I chuckled. After I showered, I got dressed in a pair of denim, stone washed rip jeans, black t-shirt and a pair of Timbs. I walked down the stairs where Kanya had the pups sitting in something that swings back and forth.

“What is that?” I asked Kanya.

“It’s a rocker; it calms the babies,” she said, tickling their stomachs.

Amadi, Elle and Izra came into the family room.

“So, who is going to discuss last night? I knew I should’ve killed Dash when we saw him and his gang at the club. That muthafucka is sneaky,” Izra fussed.

“We can discuss that later. In the meantime, people are coming here to take pictures. I don’t know how I feel about humans being in our home,” I said.

Kanya looked at me then rolled her eyes. “My parents are human.”

“They aren’t welcome neither,” Izra said.

“Don’t you start with me, Izra. I will kick your ass,” Kanya said, pushing him. Izra slid into the wall then came crashing down onto a table.

“Now, let’s get this place in order so we can get this show on the roll,” Kanya said, switching out of the living room. Elle, Amadi and Izra looked at me. “Now that is what you call a woman,” Elle said and Amadi agreed.

I looked around, making sure Kanya wasn’t around me. I blocked her from my thoughts. “I’m going to ask Kanya to marry me,” I told my pack brothers.

“We ain’t human, nigga. You and her is mated for life. That’s stronger than marriage,” Izra said.

“Her parents will be coming here for the grand opening of Beastly Treasures. In their human tradition, a man marries a woman if she gives him children. Kanya is trying to adjust to my life, and I’m trying to adjust to hers. She isn’t human, but she was raised with human traditions,” I said.

“Go for it, bro,” Amadi said.

“You got to keep your mate happy,” Elle said.

"I'm cool with it, but I'm telling you now, her parents better not come over here cooking that shit in our kitchen. What's that ugly bird called that humans be frying again?" Izra asked me.

"Chicken," I said laughing.

"I hate chicken and any other white meat," Izra said.

"Don't we all," Amadi agreed.

The buzzer rang throughout the house, letting us know that someone was at the gate. Kanya's heels clicked throughout the foyer. "I'll get it," she said excitedly.

Izra smiled. "Don't you start any shit," I warned him. Amadi and Elle chuckled, walking out of the family room to greet the guest.

"Come on, bro. I'm not going to ruin nothing. I wanted to give you these though," he said, going into his jeans pocket. He pulled out a velvet, black box.

"What is this?" I asked, taking the box.

"Something you know nothing about, but I think we all should wear them during the grand opening," Izra said. I opened up the box, and it held a pair of gold diamond fangs. I picked it up examining it. "Yo, what can I do with this?" I asked Izra. He took his out of his pocket and opened his mouth, extracting his fangs from his gums. He placed the teeth over his fangs, top and bottom row.

"These are called fronts. This shit is hitting. I was creative with this shit, wasn't I?" Izra asked me.

"You made those?" I asked him.

He smirked. "Yup." I put mines into my mouth. They fit snug, but they don't feel bad. I stuck my tongue out feeling the tip of the gold fang, and they were sharp. Kanya walked into the living room. "Goon, this is the camera crew and the make-up artist," Kanya said with a whole entourage behind her.

"What's up?" I asked them.

"What on earth is that in your mouth?" Kanya fussed.

"I freaking love it! Amanda, go and fetch me my camera out of the van. Jessica, go get your hair supplies. I can see this now. An urban werewolf," some white slim guy said.

"An urban werewolf. How ironic is that, Goon?" Izra asked me, chuckling.

“I can see where I’m going to go with this. I’m thinking yellow contact lenses, a ripped shirt and those heavy medallions Kanya showed me to go around your neck. I want the photo to speak for Beastly Treasures,” the slim white guy said, circling around me. I didn’t want to read his thoughts. He was feminine like Kanya. I could only imagine what his thoughts were. I wanted to hurry up and get this over with.

“No need for the contact lenses. I have my own,” I told him.

“Wow, he is hot!” I heard him whisper to Kanya.

“I’m sorry everyone. This is Anastasia, and he will be working for me with promoting our jewelry line. He will be responsible for advertisement,” Kanya said.

“Anastasia, have you seen our brother, Dayo? He has been gone for about a few weeks now, and maybe y’all clubbed together,” Izra said.

“Don’t mind him, Anastasia. He smokes a lot of weed,” Kanya told the flamboyant man. There were about eight people in our spacious family room setting up their stations and cameras. Kanya was walking around giving out snacks and drinks. I wanted these humans out of my house.

"This is a very lovely home—very huge. I haven't been in a house this big before. It almost looks like a castle," Anastasia said.

"Sorry I'm late. I got caught up in traffic," Adika said, walking in. Adika looked at me. Her thoughts weren't out of the ordinary, but she was hiding something. Akea started crying at the top of his lungs, and I saw a flash of red in Adika's eyes.

"Get the fuck out, Adika," I said to her.

"GOON! We have company, and you will not do this here. She is a part of this too," Kanya said. I grabbed Kanya by the arm, pulling her into the corner. Everyone's eyes were trained on us.

"If I tell you I don't want that bitch in my home, then that's what I mean. I can feel Akea's feelings and something bothers him every time she comes around. I can't see the image because he is a baby, but I can feel it. Adika is no good for our pups. Now get that bitch out of my house before I do it," I growled at Kanya.

She snatched her arm away from me. “I’m sick of you controlling me. Adika isn’t going anywhere. Akea is just a fussy baby,” Kanya said.

“We will talk about this later,” I said to Kanya, walking off. Adika was laughing loudly with one of the photographers. I grabbed her by the arm, pulling her out of the living room. When we got into the hallway by the door, I shoved her into the corner. “Do not come around my pups. Do you understand me? I don’t want you nowhere near my home, and if I catch you, I will bite your fucking head off.”

Adika smiled. “At your command,” she said.

Kanya walked over to us. “Adika, you will stay here like we agreed. Goon is not my father and neither is he yours. Now, go over there so Jessica can put your make-up on,” Kanya told Adika. Adika stormed off upset. “Adika was in my life way before I even knew what I was. She was here before you, and that is my friend. You will respect her,” Kanya said to me.

“Maybe your maternal instincts haven’t kicked in yet. You need to be more observant when it comes to our pups.

Adika is up to something, and it involves Akea. I will get to the bottom of this, and when I do, you better stay clear of me too. You let that bitch into our home. If something happens to our pups, not only will I hold her accountable, but I will hold you accountable too, and there would be a punishment for going against the pack," I told Kanya.

"Fuck you and this pack," she said, getting angry.

"Likewise," I said. The buzzer rang. Kanya pressed the button on the wall to open up the gate. Moments later, Jalesa came inside of the house. "I'm not good with directions. Forgive me," Jalesa said to Kanya. Jalesa looked at me then bowed her head. I gave her a head nod. At times I wondered if Jalesa knew what I was, but that would be impossible since she is human. Kanya showed Jalesa to the family room.

"Look at the twins. They are so adorable," Jalesa said. She picked Akea up out of his rocker then held him. She started humming. Akea closed his eyes, falling asleep. "Oh, wow. I'm jealous. Akea is very hard to please, almost like his father," Kanya said out loud.

Adika watched Jalesa, and I watched Adika. Adika's thoughts were blocked. She said she purposely blocked her thoughts because of Izra. She told Kanya she used some type of herb to change her scent, but I knew she was hiding something, and I was going to get down to the bottom of it. Izra said he was over Adika because she was trying to get over him, but I could see he still had feelings for her. He's like me, trying to figure out what's going on with her.

"Okay, everyone. It's time to shoot!" Kanya's assistant yelled out. Kanya went into the bathroom then came back out with gold eyes and her fangs hanging out of her mouth. Her hair was wild and bushy like a lion's mane. I chuckled to myself at how much she looked like a beast, especially with the black lipstick she had on.

"Oh wow, you don't even need anyone to do your make-up. I like that look. You make it look so natural. Even your teeth look real," Anastasia said to Kanya while touching her teeth and fluffing her hair out. "Okay, Goon and Kanya will shoot first, and then everyone else will join. Something is missing," Anastasia said, tapping his chin.

"Got it," Anastasia said, ripping Kanya's black t-shirt up. Her bra was showing and so were the tattoos on her back. "Now this looks edgy," he said. Kanya and I stood in front of a white background.

I've never taken a picture before, so don't expect for me to be with all of this. That little prissy friend of yours better not take more than five minutes, I said in Kanya's head.

You are ruining my moment. First you insult my friendship with Adika, and now you are being a jerk. I cannot wait until this is over so I can give you my ass to kiss, Kanya replied in my thoughts as she smiled.

"Okay, Goon, show those gold fangs. Give me a menacing look. Kanya, I want you to look afraid. Place your hands on his chest so we can see the designs of the bracelets and rings that you are wearing. Goon, you bend your head down like you want to take a chunk out of her," Anastasia called out.

"That's it, Kanya. Pull his gold medallion around his neck, you know, like he is a dog misbehaving," Anastasia continued to call out while Kanya and I tried different poses together. After what seemed like an hour, everyone else did their pictures with our ancient jewelry on.

Jalesa and Adika did a picture together, but Jalesa seemed as if she didn't want to be around Adika. Three hours later, everyone left the house. I was relieved because my body felt like shifting. Kanya was giving me nothing but attitude. Amadi, Izra and Elle went out. It was just Kanya, me and the twins.

*****

Kanya slammed the glass trays in the sink that she was serving snacks on. "Yo, seriously? What the fuck is your problem?" I asked her.

"I'm tired of you controlling my life. I'm sick of you making demands. I want my mate to look at me like the woman in his life and not a damn child. You have pups, Akea and Kanye, neither one of their names is Kanya," she ranted, breaking more dishes.

"Elle is going to be pissed about that. He got those from China," I told her. One hurled passed my head, crashing into the wall. "I don't give a fuck! I'm sick of all of this shit. Amilia was right. All you Alphas do is control us!" she shouted.

"Amilia? Isn't that Dash's mate? When have you talked to her?"

"That's none of your business. Are you going to tell me to stay away from her too? I'm losing my damn mind! One minute I'm so happy, and then the next I want to taste blood from a kill. Sometimes I just wish I was normal, and I still worked at the nursing home. I even had to distance myself from my parents because of what I am. I didn't ask for this; it was forced on me," Kanya said with tears falling down her face. My chest tightened up. I felt an anger I have never felt before. I was angry and I was hurt. "Are you unhappy with me?" I asked her.

Kanya burst into tears. "No, I didn't mean it like that. You just don't understand," she said, turning away from me.

I went into my pocket pulling out her ring. It was gold with diamonds in it. The ring was shaped like a pyramid. The middle of the ring had ice blue diamonds, the color of the Nile River. I placed the ring on the counter top. “I was going to ask you to marry me. I never wanted you to feel like you needed to lose a part of yourself. I never asked you to forget how you used to live. I guess you got shit all figured out yourself, and since we are being honest, I wish the gods had chosen someone who was never human. You are ungrateful just like them,” I told her then walked out of her sight.

“Go to hell, Goon!” Kanya screamed at me.

“If you keep on fucking with Adika, you will be in hell, and I won’t give a fuck about it. From now on, you can do what you want to do and mingle with who you want to. Just don’t bring that shit to our home or around the pups,” I shouted back.

“I’m going to remember that when you come sniffing up my ass because your beast cannot resist me,” she spat.

“Keep talking shit. Nobody is here with us,” I said to her. I heard the door slam. Kanya was gone, and it was just me and the twins. I picked them up and headed upstairs. Kanye was babbling, but Akea was quiet, just staring at me. I laid Kanye in his crib then sat down in the chair with Akea. I held him up looking at him; his eyes turned blue.

I saw images of a dark figure through Akea's eyes. The figure was tall with red eyes. I couldn't see his face, but a voice echoed throughout the room. "Saka," it muffled, and then Akea cried. Someone wanted my son.

Keora

"Damn it!" I screamed, knocking my spell books from off of the table. Goon could sense me now…Well, Akea could sense me. I was better off as Dayo, but as Dayo I couldn't get close enough to Akea. Getting close to Akea was a bad move; he could sense me. Saka was haunting Akea through me. Nobody could detect me but him. In Akea's eyes, I looked like a demon. My plan wasn't going to work. It was too late for me to walk away because I promised Saka Akea's soul if he made me powerful enough to defeat Naobi. Saka tricked me. He knew I couldn't defeat Naobi, but I still have to give him what he wants.

I sat on my rug in front of the fireplace. I closed my eyes then cried. Goon would never love me, especially if I gave Saka his son's soul. The fire from the fireplace blew out towards me, and a dark figure appeared. I backed up into the corner.

"Are you having second thoughts?" the ancient voice asked me.

"Saka, I cannot get close to Akea. Goon does not even want me around. Akea can see me for what I really am, and he cries every time I'm around him," I explained.

"I gave you my spells in return for Akea. I want to walk the earth again. I've been in the dark for a very, very, very long time," he said to me.

"I can't do this anymore," I said to Saka. My body was pressed against the wall. Something was choking me and burning my neck, causing me to scream out in pain.

"I gave you my spells, and I can take them away. What do you think Naobi would do to you if she could sense all of your doings? The next time I come, you better have that baby," he said. Then just like that, he disappeared.

I sat four bloody steaks on a tray with a pitcher of water. I warmed up some soup for Adika. I took the food tray then headed down to the dungeon.

"Did you two miss me?" I laughed. Adika sat in the corner with her knees bent up. Dayo lay on the hard floor on his back. I gave him some pants to wear; Adika seeing Dayo naked bothered me for some reason.

"How long have I been here?" Adika asked, looking sick.

"A week. What's the matter with you?"

"I don't feel good. Please get me out of here. This dungeon makes me feel human! Immortals don't get sick. What kind of place is this?" she yelled at me.

"What would be the point of you being in here if you could still cast a spell?" I asked her.

"You can keep me for however long you want to, but let her go, Keora," Dayo said, sitting up.

"Why do you show concern for her?" I asked him, getting slightly jealous. I couldn't help but feel this way towards Dayo because he marked me. When Dayo bit me, he connected me to him.

"Get her out of here. She is sick. If she dies, don't you die too? You are one dumb-ass witch; you don't know shit. I bet your plan is backfiring isn't it? Goon still isn't sniffing behind your old ass," Dayo spat.

“He used you, Keora. You’re never supposed to make an agreement with an evil warlock. Didn’t Naobi teach us that?” Adika asked me.

“Fuck Naobi. Don’t you mention that bitch’s name in my house. I will cut your tongue out the next time that you do.”

“I’m with child, Keora. You cannot do this to me,” Adika cried.

“WHAT!” I shouted.

“I found out around the time Izra and I broke up that I was carrying his pup. I blocked him from my mind so he wouldn’t know. If I knew you was going to do this to me, then I would’ve told him. You want me to give birth in this hell you got us in? How dare you.”

“You are lying. Only Alphas mate,” I said. Then Dayo laughed.

“How the fuck are you going to be with a werewolf if you don’t know shit about one? Alphas mating under a full moon is just a ritual, almost like a wedding. It just means that all Alphas would impregnate their mate, and they would become mates for life. If he marked her, then that means he is a mature wolf that can impregnate his mate," Dayo said.

"I don't believe you, Adika," I said to her. She stood up then lifted up her shirt; she had a slight pudge.

"Our baby is immortal; therefore, I won't stay pregnant long. Now, would you get me the fuck out of here?" she asked me.

"You know Saka loves witch and werewolf blood babies. Maybe I can use your little puppy to give me more time to get Akea," I said to Adika. She walked towards the bars until she was only a few feet away from me. Adika spat in my face. "Shame on you. Shame on you!" she screamed. Dayo ran to her to calm her down. "Get your hands off of her," I spat as he hugged her. Dayo dropped his arms from around her, his toned chest heaving up and down. My eyes traveled down to the piece he had between his legs, and my body burned with desire. I hated the attraction I had for him, and I hated how he looked me in the eyes as if he was trying to read my thoughts.

Dayo licked his lips, causing my pussy to throb uncontrollably, and my body wanted him. My body wanted to carry his pup. I shouldn't have tricked him into marking me because the urge was becoming unbearable.

Dayo

After Keora stood outside of the prison-like bars eyeing me, she disappeared. I looked at Adika who was balled up in the corner with tears falling down her face.

"I'm going to get us out," I told her.

"How? You can't shift and neither can I," she said. Adika was more attractive than Keora. She had very unique features, and her skin was the color of chocolate.

"I marked that bitch. I can see it in her eyes that her desires are uncontrollable. Let's just wait this out. I give her another week, and she will be down here trying to shove my dick down her throat," I told Adika, and she laughed, wiping her eyes.

"You almost sounded like Izra. I miss him so much. I shouldn't have broken up with him. I just wanted him to appreciate me," Adika said.

"We are very sexual creatures. You know what humans say about animals? They say all animals do is eat, sleep and mate. We weren't designed to have all of these emotions like humans. We think of surviving in this world."

"I'm going to put all of my faith in you," Adika said to me.

"I want to go home too. I miss my brothers. I don't know what that bitch been doing, but I'm sure they probably hate me. I can see Izra bad talking me now," I laughed.

"Why wasn't you and Izra getting along?" Adika asked me.

"We are too much alike. We bump heads a lot, and Goon defends him like the older brother. Goon and I use to fight every day years ago. He use to beat my ass too. His beast is too strong, and I don't think he even knows it," I said, thinking about my brothers.

"Did Amadi get any pussy yet?" I asked Adika.

"I see why you and Izra bumped heads a lot; only he would ask me some nonsense like that."

"Amadi fell in love with a human woman. He tried to mark her, but his bite killed her. He kind of stayed to himself after that. Those oils he makes are because of her. She taught him how to make them," I told Adika.

"You really miss them, don't you?" Adika asked me.

"Yes, I do. I miss them all, even the pain in the ass, Izra. That motherfucker pissed on my boots months back. He got some serious issues, but that's my lil bro," I said. I didn't have a plan, but I knew I had to find a way out of the dungeon.

Kanya

"Okay, everyone, my parents are only a few minutes away. Can y'all please behave, especially you Izra," I said to him. I had a long morning and was already worn out. The twins were fussy. They slept all day and were awake during the night. Goon has been distant for the past few days. He talked to me only when he had to. I didn't mean what I said to him. I was frustrated because at times I found it hard to adjust to my new life. He was going to propose to me, and that was a lot for him to do because that was not his tradition. Goon was willing to adjust to my life, and I didn't return the favor. I have been selfish towards him the past few days, which has made me miserable. I could still see the hurt in his eyes when I told him that I didn't ask for this life and that I missed my old life. As much as I wanted to take the words back, I couldn't. Goon is very stubborn and does not easily forgive.

"Elle, is the spare bedroom clean, and does the bed have clean sheets on it?" I asked him.

"Don't worry, Kanya. I took care of everything," Elle answered. Elle and Amadi are very respectful. I was really worried about Izra being around my father; my father could be a bit much at times. I set up the kitchen table for dinner. I grabbed a few old vintage wine bottles out of the cellar.

When I came back into the kitchen, Goon was standing there with the twins dressed in cute, little outfits. Goon was wearing a white long-sleeve shirt that hugged his frame and a pair of jeans with a brand new pair of Timbs. His cologne filled the kitchen, and like always, my heart skipped a beat. The passion in his eyes spoke volumes; even if he was mad at me, I could still feel his love. I wanted him to wrap his strong arms around my body. I wasn't a small woman, but when he hugs me, I get lost in his embrace. Goon was built to be my protector.

"They are hungry," Goon said, handing me the babies.

"Shit, I been so busy, I forgot to feed them," I said. He eyed my finger. I was wearing the ring he was going to propose to me with. Even if he changed his mind, it still meant a lot to me.

"It looks nice on you," he said bluntly.

"We need to talk," I said to him.

"I'm not in the mood for any of your insults. I tolerated enough of that bullshit."

"Why are you so mean?" I asked him as anger flashed in his eyes.

"You have been acting like a bitch. All I hear is shit about you. What about me? How do you think I feel not knowing shit about myself? Have you forgotten that I have lived a thousand different lives and don't remember shit from none of them? Did you forget that I barely know my parents? Do you think it was easy for me? I don't know who the fuck I am. All I know is this pack and you. I don't know anything else beyond that, but not once have I ever regretted you. I don't even think about that shit. You said some shit to me that fucked my head up. You got me doing human shit, and I don't mind it because it makes you happy." Goon stormed out of the kitchen as I followed behind him.

"Did you just call me a bitch?" I asked him.

"Aren't you a female dog?" Goon replied smartly. I gave Amadi the twins when he walked down the stairs.

"Come on, Kanya. Your parents will be here shortly," Amadi said to me.

"Fuck that. I want this son of a bitch to get off whatever it is he has on his chest," I said, pacing back and forth. Goon leaned against the wall smiling cockily at me.

"You see this shit, bro? Her little beast wants to attack me. What's up, Kanya? You want to release her? Go ahead, but don't get mad when I sink my teeth into your throat," Goon threatened me. I charged into him. He caught me then put me in a restraint. My fangs pierced through his arm as I tried to escape. He grabbed me around the neck then pushed me into the wall. I could feel his nails pricking my skin. His eyes were blue and his teeth were sharpened.

"Don't fucking tempt me," he growled, lifting me up off of the floor by my throat. I slashed his face, swinging my arms wildly, causing three bloody scratches on both sides of his cheek.

“I cannot believe this shit,” Amadi said, and then he called out to Izra and Elle. Izra and Elle ran into the hallway to pull Goon off of me. Goon dropped me on the floor. “That will be the last time you try and challenge me,” he spat.

Tears welled up in my eyes. “I hate you,” I said.

“What the fuck did you just say to me?” he roared. I took the pups from Amadi then hurriedly locked myself inside of the bathroom in the hallway. I sat on the toilet, breast feeding the twins, as tears fell from my eyes. I guess no relationship is perfect, even when you are with your soul mate.

After I breast fed the twins, I sat them in their rockers. I headed upstairs to shower and get dressed. I put on a cami, a cardigan sweater and a pair of jeans. I slipped my feet into a soft pair of tan moccasins. Goon came into our bedroom. He headed towards the closet to change out of his shirt that had blood on it from where I scratched him.

I got up then walked towards him. Our relationship is bipolar; neither one of us was willing to back down. Our beasts were going against each other.

"I don't hate you," I said to him while his back was turned towards me. He didn't answer me. I reached out to touch him, and surprisingly he didn't resist my touch. He put his shirt over his head then turned around to face me. "I need us back to the way we were," I said to him.

He caressed my face. "I let my beast get the best of me. It won't happen again," he said then walked out of my sight.

Few minutes later, I was standing in front of the house while my parents pulled up in their Honda CR-V. My mother was the first to get out. "There goes my baby!" she shouted with her arms out, and like a little girl I ran into her embrace. I hugged my mother for dear life. I felt normal again.

"Look at you and all of that wild brown hair," she said, playing with my tendrils. My father got out of the truck. "There's daddy's little girl. Your mother talked me out of giving you an ass whipping. For a split second, I thought you was trying to avoid us," he fussed. I wrapped my arm around him then kissed his cheek.

"I missed you too, daddy."

"This is one helluva house. What else does Akua do for a living? He isn't a diamond smuggler is he? I read articles about how the men in Africa are sending them children into those diamond mines and getting paid off of it. This house is the size of the white house," my father fussed.

"He inherited it, daddy. Please don't ruin this moment," I said, and then he mumbled underneath his breath. Elle and Amadi came out of the house.

Oh my heavens. What has God created? They are built like African warriors, my mother thought. Elle and Amadi smiled because they heard her thoughts as well.

"Mom and Dad, this is Elle and Amadi. They are Akua's older brothers," I said introducing them.

"Nice to meet you. We are glad to have you here. Do you need any help with your luggage?" Amadi asked as Elle and my father chatted away.

"This is such a beautiful home," my mother said, stepping onto the foyer.

These guys are nothing but thugs and criminals. I don't know what Kanya has gotten herself into. Why couldn't she be with a nice, young and proper gentlemen? These men have nothing but weird tattoos all over the damn place. I bet they are into some type of mafia. They are too young for a house this big. I will get down to the bottom of this. I hope Kanya is smart enough to leave when we leave. I didn't raise her to become affiliated with such people, my father ranted on inside of his head. I was beyond hurt that he would look down on people whom I considered to be like family.

"Mr. and Mrs. Williamson, glad to see you again," Goon said, coming into the foyer. He had the twins in his arms.

"Are those my grandbabies?" my mother asked excitedly. She took Kanye from his arm. "Oh my heavens, they are handsome, and they are chubby little things."

"Hand me over that little fellow," my dad reached his arm out for Akea.

"Wow, Akua, they look just like you," my mother said. Izra came into the foyer, and I started to get nervous.

"This is Akua's youngest brother, Izra," I said introducing him.

"Nice to meet you, especially this lovely lady here," Izra said, grabbing my mother's hand and kissing it.

Where did all of these nicely built, handsome men come from? my mother thought. Goon escorted my parents around the house while I stayed back with Elle, Amadi and Izra. I didn't want to hear any of my father's negative thoughts.

"Your mama got a fat ol' booty. Her scent is amazing. I'm jealous of that little father of yours. She is too much woman for him. Tell him I can handle her," Izra said. I kicked him as hard as I could.

"Watch it, jackass," I said. Elle and Amadi burst into a fit of laughter. After a while, I had to laugh myself.

Izra pulled me to the side, away from Elle and Amadi. "What's the matter with you?" I asked him.

"Can you talk to Adika for me? Tell her the games are over, and I miss her. She even changed her scent. I don't know how she did that, but those witches are always doing some shady shit," Izra said sadly.

"I thought you was over her?"

"I marked her, Kanya. I don't think I can just get over her like that. I'm tired of the shit, and I need her back. I couldn't sleep last night. Something is wrong, and I can't figure it out. Have you heard from Keora?"

"Nope and I don't want to. Adika told me the other day that Keora went back to Africa."

"I'm with Goon; something is up with them," Izra said.

"Where does Keora live?" I asked Izra.

"Nobody knows. Dayo just up and left, and then Adika started acting like a bitch. Some shit ain't right with them."

My parents and Goon came back into the foyer. "I'm all tired out, and I didn't even see the whole house," my mother said, rocking Kanye in her arms. The twins are very spoiled; even the pack brothers spoil them. I was surprised at first how attentive they were with them after I first had them.

I wonder if there are any drugs in here. Oh God, my daughter is in danger. Akua looks like a criminal. I bet he is the ring leader. She should've stayed with Jason. What happened between Jason and Kanya? my father thought.

Goon looked at my father like he wanted to hit him, and the pack brothers shook their heads because they heard his thoughts too. I was beyond embarrassed; they'd been welcoming since the moment he arrived.

"Kanya, can I speak with you for a minute?" Goon asked me.

"Is everything okay?" my father butted in.

"Yes, Mr. Williamson, I would like a word with my fiancée in private, if that is alright with you," Goon spoke sternly.

"You two are engaged? Congratulations! Did you hear that, honey? Akua will be a part of the family," my mother said to my father.

Like hell he will, over my dead body, my father thought. I got up then walked out of the family room into the hall.

"Who is Jason?" Goon asked me.

"Seriously?"

"You damn right I'm serious. Who the fuck is he, and what does he have to do with you?"

"He's my ex-boyfriend that I had been with four years. I found him with another man. After he broke my heart, I went celibate for a year, and then I met you. I have no connections with him, but he and my father are still cordial. My father doesn't know that Jason is gay."

"Your father is very disrespectful. We have been generous to him since the moment he walked his short ass into our home. I'm not taking too kindly to that." I knew this wasn't going to be a good idea. My father felt like Jason and I were better off. Jason came from a prominent family, while my father thinks nothing of Goon.

"He is very protective over me," I said to Goon.

"Is everything alright?" my father asked, walking into the hallway.

"Yes, daddy, I'm fine. Akua and I are just talking if that's okay with you," I said to him.

"Jeffery, leave them alone. We didn't come here for you to patronize anyone. Don't you start this mess again," my mother spat.

"I'm just making conversation, Stephanie," my father responded, walking back to the family room.

"I'm sorry about that, Akua. Some fathers are very protective over their daughters. In Jeffery's eyes, Kanya is still his little girl, and this all happened so quick. You two had babies, and now you are engaged," my mother said.

"I understand, Mrs. Williamson," Goon replied.

"If he bothers you, let me know. I will kick his little ass," my mother said then walked away.

"I see where you get your attitude from," Goon said, laughing.

"I'm going to start dinner," I said, walking into the kitchen. Goon grabbed my hand. "Wait a minute. You just going to leave me with your father like that?" he asked me.

"He has a Napoleon complex. Pay him no mind," I laughed, walking off.

"Hey, beautiful," Goon called out to me, causing me to smile. I loved when he called me that; it still gave me butterflies.

"Yesssss," I sang.

"I'm going to scare his little ass before the night is up. I'm just warning you now. I hope he doesn't piss in the middle of the night," Goon said then walked off.

“Arrogant asshole!” I shouted.

*****

Two hours later…

We all sat down at the dinner table laughing as we feasted on steak, rice and vegetables. My father seemed to be more interested in Elle, as they talked throughout dinner.

“So, Akua, where are your parents?” my father asked him.

“They’re in Africa,” Goon answered before taking a sip of his cognac.

“You said you are from Egypt, correct?”

“I believe I have mentioned that before,” Goon responded.

“So, my store is opening up tomorrow, and I was wondering if you two could come with me,” I said to my parents.

“Oh yeah, that’s right. I wouldn’t miss it for the world,” my mother said, kissing my cheek.

"What kind of store is it? The merchandise isn't stolen is it? I have been hearing about a gang that has been stealing jewelry," my father said. Goon choked on his cognac then pounded his chest.

One more insult and watch what I do to him. I will crawl up the highest building with him and watch him fall off, Goon said into my head.

Cut it out. My father has always been like this, I replied back into his.

Our ancestors have been collecting jewelry for centuries. It was all passed down to us to keep. We can do whatever we want with it, but Akua wanted to give it to Kanya. We have never stolen anything from anybody; we never had to," Amadi said. My mother gave my father a menacing glare.

"I'm not going to pretend that I'm impressed with you're lifestyle because I'm not. This house is too lavish for a group of young men who, by the way, don't work. I don't see any degrees on the wall. No one at this table looks over the age of thirty, and that one right there looks to be only nineteen," My father said about Izra. The glass in Goon's hand cracked, causing his cognac to spill all over the place. Goon was beyond angry. I put my head down in shame.

"Nothing else to drink, Jeffery," my mother scolded my father.

"Oh, Stephanie, lighten up. These hardcore men can take a little joke here and there," my father laughed.

Goon slapped his hand down on the table, and the table came tumbling down on the floor. "That's enough! When I came into your home, I showed respect to you and your wife. You will respect my family, especially at my dinner table. If you have an issue, then you can get the fuck out of my house, but your wife is welcome to stay," Goon said to my father.

My father looked at me, and I had to look away from him.

"Is this the type of man you want to spend your life with? Look at him. I bet he wants to bust a cap in my ass," my father said, making Izra laugh.

"Daddy, please just stop it," I said.

"I'll be back. I need to let my dog out of the cage," Izra said, but it all went on deaf ears as Goon and my father went back and forth. My mother and I started picking up the food and plates that fell on the floor.

I heard growling come from the end of the dining room, and my eyes got big as saucers. I could not believe Izra had shifted and was now walking around our dining room. Goon smiled. "Come here, boy," Goon said. Izra sat down next to Goon panting like he was a dog.

"What on earth kind of dog is that? He is huge," my mother shrieked, hiding behind me.

"His breed is very rare. There are only four others just like him throughout the world," Goon said, patting Izra's head. Amadi and Elle held their laughter in, while I wanted to scream at the top of my lungs.

My father hurriedly stood up but ended up on the floor as Izra growled at him then leaped on him.

"AARRGGHHHHHHHHHHHHHHHHHHHH!" my father screamed with tears in his eyes. Goon roared with laughter.

"Get that dog off of my husband," my mother screamed. Izra let my father up then licked my mother's hand.

"He is very friendly, but his size can be intimidating," Goon said.

My father ran out of the dining room screaming at the top of his lungs while Izra chased after him.

"Don't run, Jeffery! He thinks you're playing fetch," Goon shouted out to him. My life was spiraling out of control. I gave Goon an evil look.

You are in big trouble, I roared inside of his head.

If it doesn't involve me entering that sweet tunnel you have between your beautiful legs, then I pass. Speaking of which, those pants you have on are tempting my beast.

Are you drunk?

Let's sneak into the hallway bathroom so I can taste you. Can I dip my tongue inside of you?

Goon then blew me a kiss as sweat beads formed on my forehead. I was able to get aroused even with the sounds of my mother screaming. My father was still being chased by an oversized wolf. Thoughts of Goon stuffing his massive member inside of me filled my head.

I can smell your arousal. You want me buried deep inside of you.

My father locked himself in a room until Izra disappeared. Amadi, Elle, my mother and I cleaned up the mess that was on the floor. Goon was giving the pups my breast milk that I had pumped into bottles. I wanted to try the bottle with them since I would be spending more time at the store.

I walked my mother to the guest bedroom. I was beyond tired. "I forgot to tell you how beautiful that ring is. I know your father can be an asshole, but I'm proud of you. If Akua makes you happy, then so be it. It also doesn't hurt that he is such a beautiful man," my mother laughed. My mother and I always had a close bond. She had always let me make my own decisions. I just wished my father was more understanding.

"Goodnight, mother. I'm so happy that you are here with me. I've missed you so much," I said, squeezing her hand.

"What's the matter, my child? Is there something you want to talk to me about?"

"No, I'm just tired," I said to her. I wanted to tell her what I was, but I couldn't.

"Get some rest. I will see you in the morning. I'm going to go in this room and let your father have it," she said, opening up the door. I headed up the stairs into our bedroom. Goon was just getting out of the shower. His member swung freely between his legs, slapping against his inner thighs.

He walked over to me then picked me up as I wrapped my legs around him. He licked my lips then kissed them. My clit throbbed and moisture seeped from between my slit. I moaned then growled. "I been wanting to do this," he said squeezing my bottom. He laid my down on our bed, and I was undressed in a matter of seconds. Goon lifted my legs up then stuck his nose into my sex.

"Damn it!" I shouted when his hard tongue entered me. I pulled the sheets off of the bed, shredding them with my nails. Goon kissed my bud then sucked on it gently. His tongue went in circles around my clit then flickered across it like humming bird wings. My pussy pulsated, and then my essence gushed out of me as he sucked faster and harder. He locked my legs down, keeping my body trapped between him and our bed. He slurped up everything that poured out of me. He rubbed the head of his dick between my slit, teasing me with it. Goon's dick pierced through my tight opening causing me to scream out. I could feel his length and width stretching me open; I could feel every strong vein in his dick. My pussy slowly sucked him in. He pulled out leaving only the head in then pushed himself further into me.

Close your eyes, he said. I closed my eyes as he thrust deeply inside of me. He pinned my legs down tighter, his nails digging into my skin.*Now open your eyes.*

When I opened my eyes, I was lying in the sand by the Nile River. The light from the moon made it look as if diamonds were floating around in the river.

"Our bodies are still home, but our minds are in Egypt," Goon whispered into my ear as his nibbled on it. He rolled over with me on top of him, his girth still planted snuggly inside of me.

"Please me," he said to me as he squeezed my breast. I lifted myself up slowly coming down on his size and rocked my hips. Goon's fangs bit his lip as the veins in his neck popped out. He gripped my bottom and pushed himself inside of me, hitting my spot. My nails dug into his chest, and tiny specks of blood rolled down into the light sand. I bucked harder, rotating my hips, and my fangs grew out. Goon thrust harder into me. His sharp nails went into my buttocks. A howl escaped my throat. I turned Goon's head to the side, exposing his neck. I leaned forward then sank my teeth into his neck, locking my jaw. He thrust upwards, causing the pressure to build up in my chest. My eyes rolled into the back of my head as I came. I bit him harder, causing him to growl as his body jerked. I pulled my teeth out of his neck, and it immediately closed up. When I looked around, we were back in our room. Goon lay stretched out on the bed. I started to panic; then there was banging on the door.

"Kanya, are you alright? What were those noises?" my father asked, knocking on the door. "I'm fine, daddy," I shouted from the other side of the door.

"What was that noise? Let me see you," he said.

"I'm sick of this shit. We can't even fuck in peace," Goon said getting up. He stepped into his sweat pants then walked towards the bedroom door. He swung the door open, and my father stood there grilling him. "What's the issue now, Mr. Williamson?" Goon asked him.

"Is my daughter alright?" My father tried to peak around Goon, but Goon's body blocked his vision. "What are you doing to my daughter, and why was she sounding like that? Is she hurt?"

"Aye, beautiful, your father wants to know if you are hurt and where that noise was coming from," Goon said smartly.

"I'm fine, daddy," I said embarrassed. I wished Goon and I were really in Egypt.

"I don't like the fact that you are screwing my damn daughter."

Goon chuckled. "Kanya, I think your father would like to talk to you about the birds and the bees." My father pushed Goon. I ran towards our bedroom door.

"Stop it! Why are you doing this to me?" I asked my father. He looked at my arm in disgust. I had hid my tattoos from my parents earlier, but my short-sleeve robe now showed off all of my tribal markings that matched my mate's.

"What on earth did you to your body? What did you do to my daughter?" My father asked, charging into Goon. Goon picked my father up by the collar on his robe, holding him up in the air. Tears ran down my face. This was not what I imagined—my father and mate against each other.

"Don't you ever raise your damn hand at me in my home," Goon's voice boomed. My father's feet were dangling, and his slippers fell off of his feet. Goon squeezed harder then tossed him into the hallway. I ran to my father and helped him up.

"Daddy, I'm so sorry," I cried.

Goon put on a shirt then a hoodie along with a pair of socks and Nike tennis shoes. He leaped over the banister, landing feet first on the first floor, then walked out of the house. My mother ran up the stairs.

"What the hell is going on now?" she asked me.

"Akua and daddy got into an argument," I said. My father stood up.

"That man is on drugs, perhaps steroids. He lifted me up into the air then leaped over the banister like a damn devil," my father fussed.

I went into our bedroom then slammed the door. I looked out of the window, and I saw a glimpse of Goon's black, bushy tale running into the woods. I tried to reach out to him, but he had me blocked; he did that when he had a lot on his mind. I checked up on the twins on the other side of our bedroom. They were still sleeping peacefully. I was surprised that they didn't wake up to the sounds of Goon and me making love. I got back into bed, but I couldn't sleep. I wanted to know what Goon was thinking. I tossed and turned until the early morning. When I finally got out of bed, I fed the twins then walked them down the hall to Elle's room. I told him I would be back. I was worried about Goon.

I put my hoody over my head then walked outside, heading straight towards the woods. I sniffed the air to see if I could detect his scent. I followed his scent trail; his scent led me to a pile of his clothes and shoes. I picked them up. “GOON!” I shouted. Deer blood filled the air. I heard growling and the sounds of flesh being torn into. I walked further into the woods where Goon was hungrily tearing into a deer.

“Goon,” I called out to him. He lifted his head up, blue eyes staring into mine. Blood dripped from his fangs. He licked around his mouth. He turned his back towards me then continued to tear into the deer. I heard the sounds of shuffling in the woods. Goon perked his head up then started growling.

“Kanya, are you out here?” My mother’s voice called out. I heard the sounds of shoes stepping on the leaves. “It’s cold out here. Come back in the house.”

Before I knew it, my mother was standing behind Goon. He was still in wolf form as he looked at her with his menacing scowl. Fear settled in her eyes. I didn’t want her to find out like this.

“Is that Akua?” she asked me.

"What? Don't be silly, Mom. That's one of Goon's dogs," I said. My mother walked slowly around Goon as his eyes trained on her.

"The myth is true," she said.

"What myth?" I asked dumbfounded.

"The son of Ammon would be reincarnated until he met his soul mate. My grandmother use to tell us that story when I was little. The myth was passed down in the family. I would never forget. They said his fur is the color of midnight, and his eyes are blue like the Nile River. My grandmother told me when you was a baby that you had the jackal blood, and the son of Ammon would find you. I thought she was crazy because she was dying when she told me; she was senile," my mother said.

"You knew all along?" I asked her.

"I knew, but I didn't think such a thing would be true. I didn't want to tell you because you would've thought I was crazy. Last night, when I held the babies, their eyes changed colors. I thought maybe it was the lights in the living room."

"Can I touch him?" she asked nervously.

"Go ahead," I said. She reached out to Goon and touched his head gently. "He is so beautiful." She looked at me. "Let me see you."

Go ahead and show her, Goon's voice said.

I took my clothes and ring off, setting it in a pile to avoid ripping them when I shifted. I crouched down. Sounds of my neck snapping and my spine cracking echoed throughout the woods. My mother covered her mouth as tears filled her eyes. My face grew out, and my golden fur pierced through my skin. I stood up on the other side of Goon. His wolf shoulders towered over my head. After we mated, my beast had gotten bigger, but Goon's beast still was the biggest; he was massive. He was the biggest wolf out of the pack. I nuzzled my head under Goon's neck, and he licked my face.

My mother touched me. I jumped on her and she screamed. When I began to lick her face, she stopped then laughed. "That tickles," she said giggling. She sat up then grabbed my face, looking into my golden eyes. "You are so beautiful."

"Honeyyyyy, where are you?" My father's voice called out. Goon went back to his meal to continue to eat while I started to panic. I hurriedly shifted back to human form. I grabbed my clothes then hid behind a tree.

My father is coming, I said to Goon.

I know he is. I could smell him when he came out of the house. I'm not letting my catch go to waste. The vultures will get to it soon, Goon replied back. He growled as he savagely tore into the deer, dislocating its body. My mother grabbed her stomach then covered her mouth. Even I felt bad for the carcass. I hurriedly got dressed. My mother was so distracted by Goon that she didn't even realize when my father reached out to her. When he saw the big, black beast tearing into what was left of a deer, he gasped.

"That's one of Akua's dogs. Kanya and I just came out to walk him," my mother said.

"There's another one? Got damn it, how big do they get? That dog is bigger than a male lion. Is he eating an animal? No wonder they are so big; they don't believe in dog food," my father said, backing away.

"Shut up, Jeffery. He is a sweet dog," my mother said.

"Like hell he is. That's it! I have had enough of this shit. Kanya, grab your things. You are coming home with us. You live in a house with thugs and wild animals. My grandchildren are in danger. If you want to stay, that's fine. Your mother and I are taking the twins where the environment is safe," he fussed.

Goon didn't like the sound of that. He stopped eating. He looked at my father then growled with blood dripping from his face. Goon charged into my father, grabbing him by his jacket. My mother screamed as I looked on in shock. Goon leaped up into a tree with my father dangling from his mouth as the smell of fresh urine permeated the air—my father had peed on himself. Goon climbed up the tallest tree then leaped down, leaving my father behind. My father was scared of heights. He screamed and cried while stuck at the top of the tall tree.

No damn body is taking my pups away from me. He is lucky that he is your father. I'm about to go shower, Goon said then walked off.

"HELP ME! HELP ME!" my father cried. A few minutes later, I was climbing up the tree. When I looked down, I could no longer see my mother. When I got to the top, my father burst into tears.

"How many of you are there?" he cried out. I grabbed him by the coat, and he punched my snout.

"Get back. Get the hell away from me," he said.

The branch under his foot snapped, and he went tumbling down a few more. He was swinging on a branch with tears falling down his face.

"Oh God, help me!" he screamed. I reached out towards him, and he struck me again. "Get back, damn it," he said. I growled at him. "I'm sorry. Please don't eat me. Please don't eat me," he begged. I leaped from the branch, causing him to fall. I then leaped down behind him, catching him by his leg. My teeth sank into his leg, but at least it would save him from the fall. After I caught him, we came tumbling down on the ground, but my body shielded him from getting hurt. My mother ran towards my father inspecting his leg.

"That damn thing tried to eat me," my father said, picking up a rock and clocking me with it. Out of instinct, my mother slapped him.

"You are a wimp. This animal saved your life," she said standing up. "Find your own way back to the house," she said walking back. I growled at my father then dragged him towards the house as he kicked and yelled. I loved my father with all of my being, but I was going to love him from a distance. He had only been visiting for one day, and my home was now in an uproar.

Elle stitched up my father's leg and treated it so he wouldn't get an infection. Elle was more like the family doctor in a way. He and Amadi could work miracles together, especially with their remedies.

"Are you okay, dad?" I asked him.

"How can you live with a bunch of savages with those babies? I'm very disappointed in you. Your body looks like a sketch book. Why on earth would you get that crap on your skin? Akua put you up to it, didn't he? His body is marked all over the place," my father fussed. Elle grabbed his medicine bag then walked out of the guest bedroom.

I leaned against the doorway. "I love you a lot, and I appreciate the way you and mom raised me. But I'm a grown woman now, and that thug that you refer to him as is my soul mate. Akua is etched permanently into my life. You can either accept it or don't, but you will respect him. This is his home, and you are a visitor. He has been generous to you. I love him, daddy. I will always love him, and I will die loving him. He is the father of my babies, and soon he will be my husband. He loves me so much, and not once has he hurt me," I said to my father.

"I will not accept him," my father said standing up.

"But you will respect him in his home," I said, walking away. My store was scheduled to open up in a few hours. I texted Anastasia telling him I would be there shortly. I texted Adika, but she didn't respond. She had been distant lately but I couldn't worry about that. My new life was spiraling out of control, and it was causing me to lose my mind.

I hurriedly showered then got dressed in a pair of black pants and a sleeveless, white, loosely hung top with a black fitted blazer. My blazer flared out at the bottom and came down to my knees in the back. I slipped my feet into a pair of black peep toe stilettos. I did my make-up and fluffed my hair out. By the time I was finished, I looked like I was ready to star in a vampire movie because of my smoky, heavy-glitter eye shadow. I stood in the mirror then turned to the side. My hips had spread, and my butt was bigger than what it was. My breasts sat up perfectly, even without a bra. Before I had the pups, my breasts weren't as perfect as they are now. Goon walked into our bedroom fully dressed and smelling good. He hugged me from the back, nuzzling his nose into my neck.

"I feel like a blimp," I said, looking at my hips.

"I don't know what that is, but I think you are perfect," he said, squeezing my hips.

"You will tell me anything," I giggled. Goon's strong hands squeezed my ass, and then he gave it a hard smack. "Umph," he said, biting his bottom lip.

"I'm mad at you," I said to him.

His handsome face smirked at me. "His small ass still walking around talking shit, ain't he? I didn't hurt him, but I did scare him. He has been disrespectful, and the thought of someone taking Akea and Kanye from me sets me crazy. Nobody is taking them away from me, not even you," he said to me.

*****

A few hours later…

Anastasia and I were getting everything together. My staff would be arriving in a few minutes. I only hired four people for the moment.

"You are a real business woman. It takes months, even a year, to open up a store," Anastasia said, prancing around.

"It takes dedication, and besides, we already had the jewelry. We just needed the staff. When Akua bought this place, it was in excellent condition," I said to him.

The door opened, and a loud chime echoed throughout the store. In walked Amilia with a scowl on her face. She'd been calling me and leaving me messages, but I haven't responded.

"Kanya, we need to talk," she spat.

"Well, I'm going to check the cases and make sure they are securely locked. Call me if you need me," Anastasia said, prancing off and swinging his short, edgy cut out of his face.

"What do you want to talk about? You want to talk about how your pack came on our territory and attacked me and my mate?" I asked her.

"I had nothing to do with that," Amilia responded.

"We are not supposed to be affiliated with each other," I said to her.

"I need the job."

"I have nothing to do with that."

"We cannot let them control us," Amilia said.

"Get the fuck out of my store before the pack gets here and picks up your scent. You are a representation of your mate. I know how heartless Dash is. Therefore, I'm sure his Alpha female is the same way. As long as you stay with that make-believe pack, you are not welcome nowhere near my store. This is our territory, and you are breaking the rules. Don't tempt me to attack you, Amilia," I warned her then growled.

"You will regret this," she said with her eyes turning green.

"When your beast wants to challenge mine, you know where to find me," I said to her. Amilia stormed off. I hurriedly took the exit that led upstairs to the top of the building and opened up the door to the roof. When I walked out, Amilia was talking to Dash. I should have known it was a setup. I should've never agreed to it. I should've turned her away when she first came for the interview. If I had told Goon what happened, saying he would have been angry would be an understatement. I wasn't ready to put my pack in danger again. Dash's pack was after our jewelry. I knew it wasn't going to be the end of them.

When I turned around, Jalesa was standing behind me dressed almost similar to me. "Oh my God, you scared me," I said to her. Jalesa was a nice girl, but she was a little unpredictable.

"I'm sorry. I saw the door open downstairs and got worried," she said, eyeing Amilia and Dash as they walked off.

"You can never trust those who will always be against you," she said to me. I looked at her trying to read her mind, and like always, she was thinking about weird things. She was thinking about flowers, and that was odd to me. Jalesa was very hard to understand.

“I’m learning that,” I said, walking towards the exit.

“Hey, Kanya,” she said, calling out to me. I turned around.“Never trust a wolf in sheep’s clothing. They will disguise themselves to get closer to you. Keep your eyes open at all times, and if something feels wrong, then that mean that it is. Even our closest friends disguise themselves. Everyone has an agenda, and it’s not always good,” Jalesa said to me.

Goon

"Bro, Kanya's daddy is about to be dinner. It's been a while since I ate a human," Izra said.

"When did you eat a human?" I asked Izra as I loaded the twins up in the back of the truck. Kanya left earlier than everyone. We were still back at the house.

"When I shifted for the first time, I couldn't catch a deer. Kofi tried to teach me, but the deer was too big. I said fuck it then ate a human. I would never do that shit again, but for Kanya's father, I would make an exception."

Amadi and Elle walked out of the house, and Kanya's parents walked out behind them.

"We really appreciate you lending your house to us for a day. After we leave the opening of the store, we will be headed home," Stephanie said to me.

“Anytime. Your company was welcomed. Kanya was very excited to have y’all here even though things got out of hand,” I said to her. Stephanie pushed Jeffrey forward.

“Apologize,” I heard her whisper to him. Izra and I chuckled because Jeffrey was cursing us out inside of his head, calling us thugs and rapists.

“I’m not happy with all of this,” Jeffery said to me.

“You don’t have to apologize. I already know how you feel about me and my brothers,” I said, getting inside of the truck. Izra got into the passenger seat. Amadi and Elle rode in a separate car, although all of us are on our way to Kanya’s store.

When we got to the grand opening, there was a long line waiting at the door for it to be opened. Izra held Akea while I held Kanye. Kanya let us into the store from the back door.

“Where are my parents?” she asked me.

“They were parking when we got out of the truck,” I told her.

“This is a beautiful place,” a familiar voice said. When I turned around, I came face to face with Adika. I looked at Akea, but he was asleep in Izra’s arms.

“Awww, look at him while he’s asleep with his little lip poked out. Let me hold him, Izra,” Adika said to him.

“Have you lost your damn mind? If he asleep peacefully, why would you want to hold him?” I asked her as Kanya growled at me.

“I need to holla at you about something,” Izra said to Adika.

“What do you need to talk about?” she snapped at him. Kanya took Akea away from Izra so he and Adika could talk. He grabbed her by the arm, and then they walked away.

“Okay, everyone, let’s get to the stations,” Anastasia yelled out at the staff.

“Where did you find him at again? He is too animated. Don’t you think?” I asked Kanya and she laughed.

“He advertised himself on the internet. I met with him, and I liked what I saw. He is amazing, and he gets the job done," she bragged. Moments later, Kanya was opening up the door and welcoming the crowd in. I was glad that she was happy, but I wasn't a people person. I wanted to leave. When her parents came in, I stayed clear of her father.

"How do you think this necklace would look around my neck?" a woman asked me, pointing to a blue and yellow diamond necklace.

I hope he isn't here with anyone. Look at his tall body and nicely built arms. I bet he could pick me up and wrap me around him with those strong arms, the stranger thought.

"Would you like to try it on?" Jalesa asked the stranger, standing behind the showcase.

"Of course," the stranger answered. I walked away and noticed Kanya's eyes staring into mines. I smirked at how jealous she could be.

Izra pulled me to the side. "Bro, something is not right with Adika. I don't think that's Adika."

"I been thinking that too," I said to him.

"I did a sniff test on her."

"You put your nose in her pussy? When did this happen?"

"I took her in the bathroom. She and I started arguing. I ripped her panties off, cocked her legs open and picked her up so my nose could be eye level with her pussy. Then I sniffed her," Izra said.

"What were your results?" I asked him, chuckling.

"Another wolf has been inside of her. When I asked her who was she fucking, she ran off."

"So, why do you think that's not her?"

"I thought about everything. I marked Adika. Another wolf is not going to fuck her with my scent. Some shit ain't right, and I'll bet my life on it."

"Weird shit didn't start happening within this pack until I met Keora. I have an idea she is behind this. Then the fact that I saw something through Akea's eyes is all the proof I need."

"Does Kanya know about that?" Izra asked me.

"Not yet. I need to get to the bottom of this. Kanya isn't even sure of herself being a beast. She has too much to adapt to, and if I tell her about a demon, she won't be able to handle it. She had to go through so much in a short period of time. But once I figure out what Adika is up to, I will tell her."

A few reporters came in to snap shots of the uniquely designed jewelry.

"Where does Keora live?" Izra asked me.

"I don't know yet, but I will figure it out. Whatever it is they're up to involves Akea. I can sense it," I told him.

"Haven't you grown into a remarkable man," a voice said to me. When I turned around, it was the woman that I saw and spoke to in my dreams. Kanya told me that my mother visited her one day at her store and that her presence was very strong. This was my first time seeing her in person. I looked around to see if my father was in the crowd.

I bowed my head down to her and so did Izra. "There is no need for that," she said in a heavy, strong accent.

"I need to speak with you, and it has to be quick. My time on earth is limited," she said, pulling me away. A few costumers stared at my mother because of her long, gold gown and the gold wrap she had around her head. In the middle of her forehead was a blue diamond, and the jewels she wore looked to be heavy. She definitely stood out from everyone else in the store. She pulled me to the corner as she looked around. It was my first time seeing her in person other than the visions I saw of her. She didn't seem to have come down for a friendly visit; it seemed to be urgent.

"I'm sorry, son. I would like to stay longer, but I wore out my stay when I was taking care of Xavier. I came to warn you of Saka," she said to me.

"Who is he?" I asked her.

"He is my father."

"What does he want? I saw his figure through Akea's eyes. Why does he want Akea?"

"Akea has his bloodline; it skipped Kanye. Akea is going to be more of a warlock than a wolf when he gets older. He has wolf blood, but he isn't going to be a shifter. Saka needs his soul. He craves warlocks with traces of wolf blood inside of them. The combination makes him stronger. One of the sisters brought Saka back to life, even though I put him away ages ago. One of the sisters needed to become powerful, so she took Saka's ancient spell book in return of Akea."

"In other words, Saka wants my pup. He isn't getting my damn pup," I growled.

"We have to stop him. He is very powerful, and if he gets ahold of Akea's blood, I wouldn't even be able to battle him on earth. Me on earth is like a human on the moon. I shielded myself with a spell to protect myself on earth. I need to find a way to stay on earth longer. In the meantime, you have to figure out which sister is behind this before Saka returns in a physical form," she said to me. She kissed me on the cheek. "You are very handsome like your father. I see more of him in you every time I look into my visions of you. You were a warrior ages ago when you lived in our kingdom in Egypt, the son of Ammon. Even though that's in your past life, you still are that warrior. Your father is angry with me. He wants you to fight your own battles. I know that you can, but as your mother, I feel the need to protect you. I have to go now. I will see you soon. I may not be here in body, but I am watching you in spirit." She walked away from me then disappeared into the crowd.

Izra walked over to me then patted my shoulder. "Bro, your mother is beautiful. I always wanted to know what my parents looked like," Izra said. Elle, Izra, Dayo and Amadi were born in the immortal world—Anubi. They were sent down with Kofi without memory of who they came from. Kofi told us they were only born to guard me.

"Kofi is your father. He raised all of us to be great wolves," I told him. I watched Kanya mingle in with the crowd. Her parents had the twins. Amadi and Elle were flirting with a few women. I smiled because it was time for them to get out into the human world more. We had to adapt and get use to human ways of living. This was our home whether we wanted it to be or not.

Izra and I have a few things to take care of. I will see you later, I said into Kanya's thoughts.

What happened? Is everything okay? I saw you talking to your mother. I was on my way over but she just disappeared. Does this have something to do with her visit? she replied back while showing a couple a bracelet.

Yes, she couldn't stay long. Good luck, and by the way, you look sexy strutting around in your establishment, I said to her, and then she smiled.

Thank you for giving me all of this and so much more, she said.

Izra and I drove home to park the truck. He and I shifted then headed through the woods in search of Keora's home. I didn't know where it was, but I wasn't going to stop until I found it.

*****

A few hours later…

Izra and I were still running deeper into the woods. I remember the woods from when I was a little boy and getting lost for days. Once you was in, it was hard to come out.

Nigga, I'm tired and hungry, Izra growled.

You should've caught that deer we saw moments ago, I said to him.

I heard something, a rustling in the bushes. Izra and I leaped up into a tree then watched the figure moving around. It was night time, and the only light that shed into the woods came from the moon and the stars.

Kanya's sweet voice echoed throughout my head asking me where I was. I couldn't answer her; I was too distracted by the noise. A figure stepped out of the bushes with a black hooded cape on. She moved swiftly throughout the woods. She moved around like her feet wasn't touching the ground.

That's a witch, I told Izra, but his eyes were closed. He had fallen asleep. He went crashing down to the ground, alerting the witch.

Muthafucka, I ought to bite your ass. Get the fuck up! I shouted into his head. The witch turned around. I leapt out of the tree, jumping on her.

"Get off me," she squealed. Her voice sounded familiar. When she stood up, she uncovered her head—it was Jalesa.

"I'm on your side," she said out loud. I knew she was different, but I didn't expect her to be a witch.

What are you doing roaming around in the woods? I asked her.

She read my mind. "I was sent to keep an eye on things for Naobi. I have been following Adika ever since I met her at your home the day of the photo shoot," Jalesa said in the same accent as my mother.

What do you know? I asked, coming towards her. She backed up; many fear my beast. Jalesa was terrified.

Nigga, do you not see how scared she is of your huge, black ass? Back up away from her so she can tell us what is up with the sisters. I'm hungry and I'm tired, Izra said into my thoughts.

Would you shut the fuck up? Warrior my ass. Someone lied to us. I don't know what kind of warrior you are," I said to Izra. Izra growled at me, but I stood up firm and tall daring him to attack me. He huffed then stepped back with a bow of his head.

Jalesa tried to creep away, but I pulled her back by her cape with my teeth. *Not so fast. If you been following her, then that means you know where she lives. Show us or else I will have to answer to the gods about how you came up missing,* I said into her thoughts.

"It's a few miles away from here by a small lake. It's a pretty white house with black shutters. It looks like it doesn't belong in the woods," she said.

You are coming with us. I tossed her on my back. She held on to the fur on the back of my neck. I leaped up in a tree then took off with Izra following behind me. We jumped from tree to tree until we came across her house. We sat and watched her house. Her house did stand out amongst everything else.

"She isn't home," Jalesa said.

How do you know? I said

"When she isn't home, the house is very dark inside. When she is home, you can hear her chants from outside of the house. There would be a dark cloud cast over her house, which means she is talking to Saka."

I leaped down onto the ground, and Jalesa hopped off of my back, falling down. "You couldn't kneel down low to the ground?" Jalesa asked me.

Be thankful I didn't drop you out of the tree. This isn't Anubi. Only one who gets royal treatment is my mate.

"Your attitude is worse than Ammon's," she said, brushing her clothes off. I charged into the window of the house. In the living room area, there were a lot of candles and weird drawings on the floor. She had Egyptian paintings on the wall with potions all over the shelves.

What the hell has this bitch been doing? I asked myself.

"This is where she practices her spells," Jalesa said, appearing inside of the living room. "I have been in here a few times when she isn't home. I couldn't find anything out of the ordinary, but I sensed a spell in this house. She is hiding something with a spell casted over it."

Izra scratched behind his ear with his hind foot. *I think a tick got on me from being in the woods too damn long,* he thought to himself. I pushed him out of the way, and he fell into a shelf, knocking it over onto the floor. There was a hidden door behind the shelf. I could tell by the way the pattern was off. Jalesa slid the door back, and it revealed a long stone staircase that led to darkness. It was freezing cold. *This bitch has hell in her house?* Izra thought.

Jalesa grabbed a candle, and we walked down the long staircase. It seemed as if we had been walking forever. When we got to the bottom, it was pitch black. A familiar scent filled my nostrils; it was Dayo. Adika had that scent on her, but it wasn't as potent; it wasn't noticeable until now. She must have tried to get rid of it but couldn't.

"Is someone there?" a voice asked. The voice sounded weak. Jalesa held the candle up higher. Behind a cage, there sat Dayo and Adika. Dayo had hair all over his face, and he wasn't recognizable, but the markings on him gave him away. Adika stood up with a bulging stomach. Her clothes were filthy, and she looked sick.

No wonder you have been tired. Adika is carrying your pup, I said to Izra.

"They used this type of prison ages ago for immortals that committed crimes. It blocks your mind so you can't get in contact with others. It also strips you of your powers. No wonder you couldn't find them," Jalesa said. She started chanting, and her feet raised off of the floor. Her locks turned white and so did her eyes.

Bro, why does she look like Storm off of X-men? Izra's voice came into my head. Adika started whimpering, and Izra started howling. Dayo ran to Adika. "You all have to hurry up. Her being in here is making her body weak. The baby she is taking a lot from her. She hasn't been eating properly," Dayo said, holding on to Adika. Izra didn't look too fond of the bond Dayo had with Adika.

Why is this nigga holding on to my mate like that? If I sniff her and she smells like this nigga, I'm going to kick his ass, Izra thought. Jalesa was still chanting.

Where the hell are you? Kanya's voice came into my head.

I will explain to you when I get home, I responded back to her. Izra paced back and forth growling and huffing, waiting on Jalesa. Dayo was cradling Adika as she whimpered in pain.

The iron rails disappeared, and they were free. Jalesa fell down onto the floor. That spell was too much for her; it drained her. I helped her onto my back while Dayo carried

Adika in his arms, and Izra growled at him. We had a long journey back home.

Hours later when we got home, Kanya, Amadi and Elle were waiting around. Kanya growled when she saw Dayo walking into the room and Jalesa draped over on my back.

"What is going on here? And who is that?" she asked, pointing at Dayo. He had hair all over his face and was in need of a shave.

I shifted into human form. Jalesa gasped then covered her eyes. I put my hand over my dick, but the scowl on Kanya's face let me know she wasn't too pleased. "That's the real Dayo and Adika. Keora had them locked away in a prison while she pretended to be them," I answered.

"Bro!" Amadi and Elle called out. They ran to Dayo, picking him up.

"It feels good to be home," Dayo laughed. Elle ruffled his hair.

"You look like a wolf man," Amadi said. I hurriedly went upstairs to grab a pair of sweat pants. Izra was still standing in the living room naked. He rubbed Adika's stomach as she lay on the couch sweating. Kanya and Elle were placing cold rags on her forehead.

"What the hell is this circus of a mess?" I heard a voice coming from behind me. There stood Kanya's father in the entry way of the living room with a scowl on his face.

I forgot to tell you that their car broke down, so they will be staying another night, Kanya said to me.

"Stephanie! Get in here. Our daughter is about to indulge in some type of weird group sex," Jeffery said, staring at a naked Izra.

"Damn it, Jeffery. What is your problem now?" Stephanie asked, coming into the living room. She covered her mouth when she noticed a naked Izra.

Oh my heavens, he is hung like a stallion. He doesn't look a day over twenty years old, Stephanie thought.

"Damn it, Izra. Put some clothes on will you!" Adika screamed then threw a pillow at him. Izra walked past Stephanie and Jeffery nonchalantly.

"What's the matter with her?" Kanya asked worried.

I saw the worried look on Elle's face when he stood up. "What's the matter?" Adika asked, trying to sit up.

Dayo told her to relax. Izra hurriedly came back downstairs, running to her side. She cried when he hugged her.

"I think she needs to go to the hospital," Stephanie said.

"There isn't a hospital for our kind," I told her.

"You all are wolves?" she whispered to me.

"And witches," I answered her.

"I'm calling 911! I will not be responsible for you thugs giving a pregnant woman a date rape drug," Jeffrey fussed.

"Shut the fuck up before you become dog food!" Izra shouted at him.

"Everyone calm down," Kanya said nervously.

"How many months is she? When I saw her earlier, she didn't look pregnant," Stephanie said.

"It's a long story," I told her.

Elle walked over towards me then pulled me to the side. "What's up?" I asked him.

He looked over his shoulder. “How do we tell Izra that his pup is dead? Adika is carrying a dead pup,” Elle said sadly.

“How do you know?”

“Immortal babies’ hearts beat loud and fast. When Kanya was pregnant, we heard the heartbeat even when we stood next to her. Adika’s pup doesn’t have a heartbeat.”

“Izra’s heart won’t be able to take that,” I said to Elle.

“You tell him while we take her to the basement. We have to get the pup out of her. That’s what is making her sick.”

“I thought immortals doesn’t get sick.”

“We don’t, but the prison Adika was in made her weak, stripping her from her nature. It’s almost like she became human when Keora locked her away. Those prisons make immortals feel pain that they have never endured before,” Elle said, walking away.

Everyone helped with escorting Adika to the basement while I grabbed Izra’s arm to keep him from going.

“I have to talk to you. Walk outside,” I said to him.

“Not now, bro. I have to stay with Adika,” Izra replied.

"I would never get in the way of that, but this is important."

When we walked outside, Izra was quiet. "My pup is dead, and I already knew that. I knew that when I first saw her," he said with water falling from his eyes. He touched his face looking at his fingers.

"Those are tears, bro. I didn't know we could feel that until I met Kanya," I said to him.

"This shit hurts. I didn't know she was locked away. I treated her like a piece of ass, and this is all she ever wanted," Izra said then sat down on the step. A loud scream pierced our ears; it came from Adika.

Izra's clothes shredded as he shifted right before my eyes then ran towards the woods. Moments later, I heard a hoarse howl. Kanya came out of the house with blood on her clothes. It was Adika's blood from when they removed the pup.

"I don't know what to do," she said as she burst into tears. I wrapped my arm around her shoulder, pulling her into me. "All she wanted was to feel normal," Kanya cried.

Dayo came outside with blood on his clothes too. “It was like hell being locked away in that dungeon. I feel like it’s my fault. I told her I was going to get us out, but I couldn’t,” Dayo said sadly.

“If we get rid of Keora, Adika dies with her,” Kanya said.

“Keora needs to be locked away for eternity,” I said.

“I didn’t think my coming home would be so pitiful. I thought I was going to come to celebrate with my brothers. I wanted to catch a nice fat deer then sleep in my bed, but this house is filled with sadness,” Dayo said. I stood up then gave him a brotherly hug.

“I’m glad you are home so I can have someone’s ass to kick. When all of this dies down, we will have a great celebration. I’m glad to have you back,” I said to him.

“Keora told me Kofi went back to Anubi. Is that true?” Dayo asked me.

“Yeah, and once you go back, it’s hard to come back out. Once you come out, it’s hard to go back. That’s some screwed up shit,” I said. I wished Kofi was still here, especially for Izra. Izra is bull-headed and holds grudges for a long time. I had a feeling that he wasn't going to be the same. Unlike the rest of us, Izra didn't fully understand things. He was still what we call a "young wolf." He was carefree, but when life got serious, he didn't understand. I was like Izra until I met Kanya. Being with her opened up a lot of parts of me that I didn't know existed. I experienced more emotions then I could count.

"Izra is going to be in the woods for days in wolf form. You know how stubborn he gets," Dayo said.

I wiped Kanya's tears away. How she felt about Adika is how I felt about all of my pack brothers. We might not all get along all the time, but we are bonded spiritually.

"Your father needs to be out of this house by morning. Izra isn't a tamable werewolf and can be pretty vicious. I don't want to have to bite him to calm him down. He has been through enough," I told Kanya.

"That is bullshit, Goon!" Kanya shouted.

"Like hell it is. Do you not see how he provokes us? We are fucking wild beasts! Once we shift, that's pretty much it, so if you don't want his little ass ripped apart, then I suggest you tell him to leave. He can stay at the best hotel in town on me," I said to her. Kanya got up then stormed into the house.

"Mates need to come with some type of instruction. One minute she tries to challenge me, then she gets jealous, and after all of that she wants me to fuck her brains out," I said.

"Interesting," Dayo laughed.

"Bro, you need to shave and take a shower. You smell like you been in a jungle," I laughed.

"You are still a cocky muthafucka," Dayo said. I stood up, ready to go in the house to check up on Adika and to let Kanya have her few minutes of being complicated.

"So, a witch took pleasure from you?" I asked Dayo because Keora had Dayo's scent.

"Yeah, she did. If she wasn't an evil bitch I might've enjoyed it more. An evil witch with a magical pussy is a deadly combination I learned," Dayo said.

When I walked into the house, I heard Kanya's father whispering on the phone. My ears could hear a mouse running in the field miles away.

"Yes, they have a dead body down in their basement. She is my daughter's friend. They killed her! They cut her stomach open and pulled out her baby while she was fully awake. I fear for my life," he told the 911 operator. I grabbed Kanya's father up off of the couch, raising him high up in the air. My eyes turned blue when I stared him in the eyes, and he looked on in horror.

Give me the fucking phone, I spat angrily inside of his head. His hand shook when he gave me the phone. I snatched it from him with the sound of his muscle cracking. "Tense aren't we?" I asked him.

"Hello, is anyone there?" the operator asked.

"My wife's grandfather has dementia. He didn't mean to call," I told the lady over the phone, and she laughed.

"No need to worry, sir. I doubt a woman being cut apart like that would still be alive," the woman replied. After she hung up the phone, I crumbled it into pieces then dropped him on the floor.

"As much as I love Kanya, I will not continue to tolerate this bullshit. Now, you either can stay out of my way or stay in a hotel," I said to him.

“What are you?” he asked me.

“Prince charming,” I said chuckling, walking away towards the basement. When I walked into the room, the smell of blood permeated the air. Amadi was giving Adika an herbal drink to get rid of the weakness. She looked at me then faintly smiled.

“There’s the beast man,” she said to me.

“Can you guys excuse us for a second? I need to talk to Goon alone,” Adika said to me. Jalesa, Amadi and Elle all exited out of the room. Adika sat up in bed. She had lost some of her color. Her lips were dry and her skin looked pale.

“You have to kill me,” Adika said.

“What?” I asked her.

“That’s the only way to stop Keora. You’ll have to bite my neck. Your bites are more deadly than everyone else’s in the pack. It would be a painful but quick death. If anyone else bit me, I would suffer.”

“Have you lost your damn mind? I’m not doing that shit. Your body just went through a lot, and I’m sure when Keora locked you away you lost some of your mind. Kanya would kill my ass, and Izra would probably stay in wolf form for the rest of his life. Izra doesn't know how to deal with shit like this. Do you understand how hurt he would be?"

"If I could kill myself, I would. You are the only one, and I need you to stop her. Saka is using her, and even if Keora doesn't want to do it, she has to. She bought him back, so he is leeching onto her. Saka wasn't always like this; he was a nice man until he started practicing dark spells. The Egyptians loved him, but when Naobi had you, his thirst for power got stronger. He killed tons of people ages ago. He is very dangerous. Keora is his only link. If you kill me now, it will cut off his source," Adika cried.

"Do I look like a punk-ass man to you? I'm going to defeat him—me and my pack brothers. Killing you is an easy way out, and we don't take the easy way out. Now, get some rest, and let's forget about this conversation," I said then walked towards the door.

"I hope you are familiar with the warlock side of you because you are going to need it. When you use your warlock powers while you are in wolf form, it makes you very powerful. The combination is deadly. Also, tell Izra to get his ass in here to hold me. How dare he roam through the woods when I need him to console me," Adika said cracking a smile.

"You got a heart like a lion; you are very strong," I said to her.

"I have been around many years. I have seen things you couldn't imagine. I have been pregnant before…many times. They always died in my womb, but how can I give birth when birth wasn't given to me? I was created from spells to protect Ammon's kingdom ages and ages ago. That was my only purpose in life. At least I can love. That is the only emotion I have that makes me feel close to normal," Adika said.

I nodded my head then left out of her room. When I got to our bedroom, Kanya was getting out of the shower. I checked on the twins, and they were sleeping peacefully. They were only two months old. They looked like human babies, but all that will change when they turn ten. They will become immortal, and on their eighteenth birthday, their aging will start to slow down.

"You don't have to be mean to my father," Kanya said to me.

"Your father doesn't have to be a punk-ass nigga," I said.

Kanya's eyes widened. "You said nigga?" she asked me.

"That slipped out, but seriously, he needs to go. He is not a real man. He doesn't have strength, and he tends to talk a lot of shit then get scared. Your mother is more dominant than your father. He needs someone to toughen him up, wrestle with him perhaps, choke slam him here and there. He is a coward, and if you wasn't a beast and I attacked you, he wouldn't do shit about it. That is why I don't have much respect for human men. They think knowledge is the key to everything. They need to be strong protectors of their families and fighters," I told Kanya.

"One slam from you would kill him," Kanya said.

"Go to sleep, Kanya. I'm not discussing this matter anymore with you. I'm not going to hurt him. I'm trying to make him strong. I could carry your father inside of my mouth like he's a rabbit," I said chuckling.

Kanya

I sat on the bed watching Goon throw his head back in laughter because of my father. "You are just mad because you don't know who your father is," I said to him, making him laugh even harder.

"Damn, I needed that laugh," he said, pulling down his sweatpants.

"I told Jalesa she could stay in one of the guest rooms. It's too late for her to travel through the woods. Dayo is really nice, the complete opposite from what Keora portrayed him to be. He reminds me of a mature Izra," I told him.

"That's why they don't get along. I hoped that with Dayo being gone it would bring them closer. Izra, didn't seem too fond of Dayo tending to Adika. Dayo said he has been locked away with her for two weeks, and she was the only person he had contact with," Goon said.

"Do you think Dayo caught feelings for her?" I asked, getting worried. More furniture was going to be broken, and more holes were going to be in the wall. Elle and Amadi might just give up on fixing things and just leave.

"No, he just has a connection. We wouldn't betray one another like that," Goon said.

*****

The next day…

My mother was cooking breakfast while my father sat down at the table reading the newspaper.

"Good-morning, beautiful. Our car will be fixed in a few days," my mother said.

"I like having you two here, but Akua said you could take one of the vehicles. He isn't materialistic, so he won't mind if you can't bring it back," I told her.

"Now, Kanya, you know I cannot do that," my mother said, flipping over the bacon.

"So, sweetheart, what belongs to you besides the twins? Every time I turn around, Akua bought this or he bought that. I always taught you to have your own and not to depend on a man that isn't your husband," my father said, looking over the newspaper.

"Daddy, I understand you're concerned, but my well-being is the least bit of your concern. Like I stated before, Akua and I are bonded for life. What's his is mines and what's mines is his. We are never breaking up, no matter what. We are bonded for life," I told my father.

I need to get out of this house. That son of a bitch got my daughter brainwashed. I know they killed that baby last night. I will figure out what they did to it," my father thought.

Goon walked into the kitchen dressed professionally. His slacks fitted him perfectly, and his blazer hugged his solid muscled arms. My face dropped and so did my mother's. Goon always wore urban attire, such as jeans, Timbs and hoodies. His diamond watch sparkled throughout the kitchen, and his cologne tickled my nose.

That wonderful scent that seeps from out of your pussy is overpowering that disgusting smell of that greasy, fat animal your mother is cooking, Goon said into my thoughts.

I thought wolves liked pigs. Remember the story of the three little pigs and the big bad wolf? I replied back while I poured my father fresh orange juice.

Don't offend me, beautiful. You know I hate pork just as much as I hate chicken, he said, and then I burst into laughter. Goon wrapped his arms around me, and his tall body towered over mines. I was lost in his embrace. He kissed my neck.

"Awww, look honey. Remember when we were young and in love like that?" my mother asked my father. He looked at Goon and me with a scowl on his face.

"If you need me at the store, call me," I told Goon. He kissed my mother on the cheek on his way out of the kitchen.

"I'll see you two later," Goon said to me and my mother. He didn't look too happy. I had to talk him into going to the store for me so I could stay home with Adika. He finally agreed when I wrapped my lips around his dick.

Dayo came into the kitchen with only some sweatpants and house slippers on. Dayo was chewing on a big piece of raw meat. My mother adjusted quickly, knowing that she was surrounded by immortals. My father was still in the dark; a person like him would never understand. He might end up in a mental hospital. "Excuse me, young man, but aren't you going to cook that?" my father asked disgusted.

"Do we cook pussy, or do we hit it raw?" Dayo asked my father. My mouth dropped, and I wanted to charge into him. Beads of sweat started to form on my forehead.

Calm down, Kanya. Dayo can get out of hand at times, Goon said in my thoughts. My mother looked at Dayo. My father would've been red if he was a white man.

"Dayo, these are my parents. Have some respect," I spat.

"They know what fucking is, and tell pops to close his mouth. He is panting like a hyena," Dayo said then walked out of the kitchen. Just my luck. I didn't like the real or the fake Dayo.

“That’s enough of this shit! These thugs have no home training. Stephanie, pack your shit. We are catching a train!” my father shouted as Dayo came back inside of the kitchen.

“I apologize for my rudeness. A nigga been in prison for a few months. I just came home last night, and I was so hungry that I went hunting for a deer. Instead of me cooking it, I just ate the muthafucka,” Dayo said.

“See, Jeffery, the man has been through a lot. At least he apologized,” my mother said to my father. My father stormed out of the kitchen. I hated to admit it, but Goon was right; my father was a bit too much.

“I don’t think he is used to having humans in his home, Kanya. Don’t expect them to behave when that’s not in their nature,” my mother said to me.

Do I expect too much out of my pack brothers? I asked myself.

“Your mother knows?” Dayo asked me, and I shook my head “yes.”

"Have I told you how beautiful you are? Nice and plump, almost like a sheep," Dayo said then, causing my mother to blush. Elle came into the kitchen.

"Cut it out, Dayo. You still haven't learned have you?" Elle asked Dayo. Dayo shrugged his shoulders. I grabbed the tray my mother prepared for Adika then headed downstairs into my old room.

When I opened up the door, Adika was laying down floating up in the air. "Damn it, you scared me. You reminded me of that movie *The Exorcist,"* I said to Adika.

"I was meditating. I'm worried about Izra. He hasn't come back yet. I tried to reach out to him, but he didn't respond. Izra is very hard to communicate with sometimes. It's like he gets it, and then he doesn't get it," Adika said, chewing the bacon.

"You know, I met a bigger asshole than Izra, and its Dayo. I'm going to search for an apartment later. I don't think I can deal with all of this. I don't understand why Goon, the pups and I just don't all live alone together," I said.

“Wolves live in packs. It has always been that way. The Alpha takes his pack everywhere he goes. You know Goon has temper issues. I hope you get that thought out of your head because you know he always pops up.” Adika then got a look of sadness on her face, and all of a sudden, she burst into tears. “They buried my baby this morning, and I wish I could reincarnate her, but I can’t. You can only reincarnate a person if they have lived,” she said, wiping her eyes. I rubbed her back.

“You can share the twins with me,” I said, not knowing what else to say.

“Goon wouldn’t like that.”

“It felt good saying it though. I think he would really attack me if I did,” I laughed.

“Mr. Williamson is cutting up I heard,” Adika said.

“He is upset that Jason and I didn’t get married. Jason comes from a good family. That is all he is worried about. If I told my father he’s gay, he wouldn’t believe me. He and Jason still play golf together.”

“Gross,” Adika said. Izra came into the room, and I gave him a hug.

"Hey, little bro," I said to him. Then he smirked.

"What's up?" he asked me.

"How are you feeling?"

"Better," he answered. I left out of the room so that Adika and Izra could talk. I headed back upstairs to the room Jalesa was in. I knocked on the door, and then she opened it.

"Good-morning, Kanya, I'm on my way to the store now. I'm sorry I'm running late, getting Dayo and Adika out of that cell took a lot out of me," she said.

"It's okay. I'm thankful you did, although I wouldn't have minded if you left Dayo behind," I said and she laughed.

"Where are you really from?" I asked Jalesa.

"I'm from Egypt. I was a servant. I was once a human, but I got old and died. Naobi brought me back to life with a drop of my blood she took from my body."

"How long do you have on earth before you return back to Anubi?"

"Not long. If I stay past the next full moon, I will forever be trapped on earth. It's a must that we find Keora before my time is up."

Amadi walked down the hall with oil bottles in his hand. He looked at Jalesa then smirked. She shyly turned her head away from him.

"With all of this chaos going around, I never got a chance to ask you, but can I take you out tonight?" Amadi asked smoothly. Jalesa blushed really hard then stared down at her feet shyly.

"Of course," she said. Amadi lifted her chin up so she could look into his eyes.

"I'm up here, beautiful," he said to her.

"I would love to be in your presence tonight," Jalesa answered. I wondered if that's how they ask people out on dates in Anubi. Amadi chuckled and walked away. Then a sadness came over me.

"Does he know you will be leaving soon—and for good— after this?" I asked her.

"Not yet. He is such a warrior. He reminds me of the men back at home with more of a caring side. Men back home are like machines; they are trained to be a certain way, and they don't love. Amadi is so passionate, and I have yet to get to know him," Jalesa said in her deep accent.

After Jalesa left, I took the twins to my mother then went hunting. I roamed around deep in the woods, sniffing the ground. I smelled a deer. A few miles away, there were two deer drinking water from a small pond of dirty, muddy water. I camouflaged myself with the leaves and the branches. I waited until I got a clear view of its neck. A few moments later, I charged into the deer, sinking my teeth into its throat. The other deer ran off as I wrestled my meal down to the ground. The deer's legs kicked wildly until I crushed its neck with my jaw.

"Grrrrrrrrrr," I heard a growl, and then the bushes shuffled. I sniffed the air and recognized the scent of another wolf, a wolf that didn't belong in my pack. Two wolves emerged from out of the bushes, both females. I crouched down low to the ground with my ears going back, guarding my kill. I growled showing my sharp canines.

This isn't your territory, I said into their thoughts.

We are starving, the brown wolf said into my head. She was smaller than the white and gray wolf, which was small also. I could tell that they were young wolves.

Where is your pack? You cannot hunt on another pack's territory, I said to them.

If you let us eat, we will not bother you. My daughter just turned, and she has not eaten anything, the bigger one said. I walked over to sniff them. Their scent wasn't familiar. The smaller wolf whimpered as the deer blood permeated the air. I stepped to the side then sat.

Go ahead and eat. I will sit here and watch. I don't want to leave you on my territory, I said into the bigger ones thoughts. They both savagely tore into the deer, ripping its limbs away from its body.

Dayo, Elle and Amadi leaped in front of the two wolves, circling around them and growling at them. They must have smelled their scents back at the house. I jumped in front of the two wolves growling at my pack brothers.

Why are these loners eating on our territory? Elle's voice came inside of my thoughts as he growled at them. The smaller wolf hid behind her mother. She was terrified of the three big beasts that circled around them, ready to attack.

This is a mother who needs to feed her pup. They are harmless, I responded back to Elle.

So was Keora. We cannot trust outsiders who aren't from this pack. There might be others involved who could ambush us, Elle spat angrily. The mother wolf shifted back to human form. She looked only to be twenty years old, but I knew she was older. She was the color of peanut butter, and her hair was big, wild auburn mane that came down to the middle of her back. Her nose was small and pointy, and her eyes were shaped like a crescent moon. Her cheek bones were strong. She looked like she had Indian blood in her.

"I would die before you hurt my pup," she said, standing her ground naked. She patted her daughter's head. "Its okay, baby," she told her daughter. Dayo, Elle and Amadi backed off while growling.

Continue to eat then. When you are finished, come to the mansion a few miles away through the woods. You can't miss it. You and your pup look dehydrated, I said in her head.

Goon isn't going to like this, Amadi said.

Goon doesn't have a choice. They are without shelter and she has a pup, I responded back to Amadi. Dayo, Elle and Amadi ran off.

"My name is Anik, and my daughter's name is Arya. We are the last of the Chippewa wolf tribe. We have been hunted over the centuries for our fur. My mate was killed years ago trying to feed us," she said.

Come to my home, and we will talk. Eat the deer while it's still warm, I replied then ran off.

When I made it back home, I walked to the back of the house then shifted back. I hurriedly grabbed my clothes that sat neatly in a pile then got dressed. When I walked inside of the house, I heard Goon's deep voice.I walked down the hallway then into the gym room.

"Hey, baby, you're back early," I said to him.

"Jalesa and Anastasia are taking over. I wasn't going to stand in a store all day. The thoughts of some human men should be banned. One guy came in with his wife, and all he could think about was how big my dick might be. That shit is for the birds," Goon fussed, taking off his blazer then tossing it on the floor. He took his shirt off then lay on the weight bench to lift the heavy weights. Amadi and Dayo were doing sit-ups and push-ups.

"I need to talk to you," I said to him. Amadi and Dayo left out of the gym room.

"What's up?" he asked, lifting up the five-hundred pounds like it weighed nothing. I stood watching the veins pop out of his nicely toned arms. His tattooed eight pack tightened every time he lifted the weights up.

"If you want some dick, just say it, Kanya," he laughed, putting the weight up. He sat up, and there wasn't any trace of sweat.

"I invited two loners here," I said to him. His eyes turned blue, and he stood up, towering over me.

"WHAT!" he shouted, causing me to back up.

"It's a mother and her pup. They are without shelter, food and clean water," I said to Goon.

"You invited some muthafuckas here that we don't even know? What if one of them is Keora?" Goon asked me.

"I know in my heart that it isn't Keora. She has a pup with her," I told him, and then he walked out of my face.

"This is the stupid shit that happens when I'm gone. I wasn't even gone for two whole hours, and you have another pack coming to our home," he fussed, walking into the kitchen. I followed behind him.

"They need shelter. It's about to get really cold out, and she has a little girl with her," I said to him.

"They are wolves! That's what our fur is for. Werewolves can survive out in the wild," he said.

"They are coming here and that's that!" I shouted at him.

"This isn't your damn house! This is all of ours, and if I say no, then that means no! Stop trying to go against my word. I'm supposed to protect this pack, and you are just inviting stray animals to our home. Young wolves are angry and always have the desire to kill. I bet her daughter killed a ton of humans already," Goon said, taking a shot of Henny.

"We will see about this," I said, grabbing items out of the fridge and pitchers of water.

"What are you doing?" Goon asked me.

"Making the shed a home for them until they get on their feet. Just because we are beast doesn't mean we have to act like it and turn our backs on people who need help," I said.

Goon growled at me then walked out of the kitchen. Moments later, Adika and I were both in the shed cleaning it out for the mother and her pup.

"Are you sure they are coming?" Adika asked me.

"Yes, a mother would do anything to make sure her pup is safe," I said as I laid down the thick wool blankets. After Adika and I were done, we headed back to the woods where I found them at. They were still eating, and all that was left was the head of the deer. They were even chewing the bones. They stopped then looked at us. Anik shifted back to human form. I handed her some clothes that were a little loose on her. Arya shifted to human form, and my heart almost skipped a beat; she was the prettiest little girl I have ever seen. Her big button eyes were the color of chestnut, and her hair was jet black and crimped as if she had braids and took them out. Arya's skin was the color of coffee beans, and when she smiled, she had the cutest little dimples.

Adika chanted something. Arya then stood in front of us dressed like a Bratz doll. Arya looked down at her clothes then smiled. "I never met a witch like you before. Thank you," Arya said running to Adika, giving her a hug.

"Arya is very friendly, too friendly, and often times it frightens me," Anik said."Thank you, Kanya. You have a golden heart just like your jackal." I told the two of them to follow me back to the house.

"Is this a castle?" Arya asked me.

"I think of it that way. Have you seen *Beauty and the Beast*?" I asked Arya.

"Yes, I have," she answered.

"Well, there is a beast in this castle. He appears mean, but he secretly has a good heart. All you have to do is give him a hug, and then he will turn into a prince," I said. They all laughed.

Goon walked out of the house with sweatpants on and a wife-beater. Like always, he had a scowl on his strikingly handsome face.

"This is not an animal shelter," Goon said. Arya ran to him then hugged his leg. "What the fuck?" he asked.

"Kanya said you needed a hug," Arya said to Goon. Goon looked down at her then growled, but after a while, his mood softened up. Goon picked Arya up then looked at her.

"She's somewhat cute," Goon said chuckling.

"It's okay, Anik. He means she is cute," I said to her as she growled at Goon. Goon held Arya in one of his arms.

"Y'all are working me, you know that? But Chippewa wolves have good hearts," he said, carrying Arya in his arm like she was a toddler.

"You have yourself a strong Alpha. He is from Egyptian roots. He is built like a warrior. You can always tell what tribe an Alpha male is from by his build," Anik said, making me blush.

"Interesting, almost like different breeds," I said.

"Egyptian wolves are huge. I bet he is bigger than a lion," Anik said laughing as we all walked inside of the house. When we walked into the house, the other wolves accepted Arya and Anik. I didn't know much about them, but their auras were warm and comforting. I hoped they would stay.

After Elle got Anik and Arya situated in their guest room, I headed to the bedroom. Goon was out hunting, so I took a shower then put on my lace bra and panty set. My mother was okay with the twins sleeping with her. My father was mad at everyone; he went to a room at the far end of the house. I fluffed my hair out then added dark red lipstick to my lips.

I lit the fireplace and then waited for Goon to return. I ended up falling asleep on the bear skin rug that laid out in front of the fireplace.

A moan slipped from my lips when I felt kisses going down my stomach then to my feet. I kept my eyes closed, enjoying the feeling. He stuck each toe inside of his mouth licking them. His free hand slid up my thigh. When he got to my panties, he ripped them off. My arousal permeated the air. I growled from the scent that poured from out of my wet pussy.

"Smells good, doesn't it?" Goon asked me. I tried to move but I couldn't.

"What the hell are you doing to me? I can't move!" I said, opening up my eyes. I was stretched out on the floor.

"You keep forgetting I got warlock blood. I can do a few things. Nothing fancy like Adika though," he laughed.

"Seriously, Goon, I don't like this," I said panicking.

"Calm down, damn. I'm going to make it worth your while. I'm glad we're on the rug because if not, the bed would break, and we don't want your little papa smurf upset," he said, licking up my legs. His hand slipped up to my breasts then squeezed them while his thumbs teased my nipples.

"Gooooooonnn," I panted while wetness seeped out of me.

He lifted my legs up then pulled me down closer to him while both of his hands gripped my ass cheeks. He lifted me up then nuzzled his nose into my pussy then growled loudly. My nipples were hard and erect, and I wanted so badly for him to suck them. My sex throbbed, and as intense as the sensation was, I still couldn't move. It was like my hands were tied and invisibly cuffed, and it there wasn't nothing I could do about it. I cried out when his wet tongue pierced through my opening. His teeth gently sank into my clit. Usually when he ate me out, I had to grab his head because at times it was too much. I couldn't grab his head as he licked and ate me to a point where the room was spinning. I wanted to squeeze my breasts; the torture was pleasurable.

"Let me drink it, Kanya. Stop being stingy and open up that pussy. You're clenching too tight," he said, entering one of his fingers inside of me. I released when he covered my pussy with his mouth, sucking and slurping on that sweet hole he loves so much.

"I'm cummmmmmiinnnnngggggg!" I screamed out. He held both of my legs up, raising my butt off the rug. He licked from my dripping wet pussy to my rear end. My eyes rolled to the back of my head. It wasn't even this intense when I was in heat.

He gave my bottom a firm slap. "POP! POP!" The noise echoed throughout the room. His teeth pierced through my right buttock, and I wished a black death could just temporarily come and take me.

"I can't take it, Goon," I said panting.

"You don't want the dick now?" he asked me as he rubbed his enormous head between my slippery wet slit with my bottom still raised up from off the rug.

"I need to move," I said to him as his rock hard dick squeezed its way into my tight hole. It was like stuffing an eggplant inside of a keyhole. I felt everything to the bottom off my ass stretch open as he slowly pumped inside of me.

"You better not shift," he said, going further inside of me. I felt my body changing, but I knew if it did, he would bring out his beast. He bent my noodle-like legs all the way back, making me take all of him.

Your pussy grips my dick like a glove, he said into my thoughts. I whimpered when he started moving in and out of me. Slushing sounds filled the room. He pulled out then came sailing in, causing my whole body to jerk forward.

My voice got stuck in my throat as he continuously pumped and grinded into my spot. I could feel the thick veins in his dick bulging and growing; the pressure caused a feeling to shoot up my spine. I felt like I was peeing, but I wasn't. I was squirting as Goon showed me no mercy. With every thrust my body convulsed. His nails grew out, pricking my skin. I howled at the top of my lungs as Goon continued to deep stroke inside of me. He leaned forward then bit me on the neck. I lost it then partially shifted. I could feel my neck snapping and my face protruding out into a snout. My body was still the body of a woman, but my face wasn't. I growled looking at Goon, but he was already partially shifted into a wolf. His blue eyes stared at me as he pumped into me over and over again, shooting his sperm inside of me. His dick swelled up then he growled. He was stuck inside of me. That's why he didn't want me to shift, because he would grow bigger and have a difficult time pulling out of me. My walls gripped him, milking him for everything he had. He growled louder as his dick throbbed. It was way more intense for him than it was for me. I smiled wickedly at him as he fell forward, panting heavily and growling.

Shift back, Kanya! Do that shit now before I bite you, he said. My body slowly shifted, loosening up around him. He hurriedly pulled himself out.

"Werewolves cannot fuck in wolf form. The pussy squeezes us as we grow, and that shit is unbearable. I almost bit your face off," Goon said, picking me up.

"Can you please allow me to move?" I asked him.

"Not tonight, beautiful. I actually like that I can do what I want to you. You resist my dick a lot, but you always want it. It's going to be a long night," he said, licking the inside of my ear. Goon stood in front of the window then pushed it open. The strong wind came slapping against our faces, and the fire from the fireplace blew out.

"Where in the hell are you taking me?" I asked him.

"Into the woods to see how well you do hanging upside down from a tree. You have been very stingy with giving me that treasure that you keep between your succulent thighs. You been very modest after you had the pups. Although you aren't in heat anymore, I'm still a beast that constantly craves for your pleasure. You have to make up for those times," he said in his raspy, deep voice while staring into my eyes. Goon leaped out of the window, landing on his feet, and ran into the woods with me in his arms to the darkest end.

Keora

I paced back and forth in the dungeon trying to figure out how Dayo and Adika escaped. I have been gone since Izra smelled another wolf on me. I have been in a hotel trying to soak in potions I made. Dayo's scent was still on me; I was also craving him. I stomped up the long, dark staircase. When I got to my living room, I knocked all of the potions I made off the shelves.

"Damn it!" I screamed, bursting the glass out of the windows. I fell down onto the floor with tears falling out of my eyes. I screamed as the tears burned my skin. It hurts when demons cry; we weren't supposed to because we don't feel nothing. I couldn't understand the meaning of my tears. A dark-like shadow came over me; it was Saka. I wished I never brought him back. He was a pain in the ass. All I wanted was to become more powerful than Naobi. I wanted to reincarnate Goon so he could forget Kanya.

Goon was becoming a distant memory to me; I no longer cared about him or Kanya, but I made a deal with Saka.

"Your heart is going pure again," Saka said to me.

"Shut the fuck up!" I screamed at him.

Then his creepy voice laughed. "I guess you just insulted me," he said."You owe me. I don't care about your love life."

"I wish I had kept you in hell," I said standing up. A powerful force came into my legs causing me to fall down. I screamed out in pain.

"Be careful of your tongue or else I will have it on a shrine."

"You tricked me! You knew that I could never be stronger than Naobi."

"You could never be stronger than your creator," he said to me.

"I can send you back."

"Go ahead. Then you will no longer be shielded. The gods will see everything you have done, and then it will be you locked away for eternity."

"I will do it."

“See you later,” Saka said, and then his spirit disappeared. I got up then took a shower, changing into my regular clothes. I disguised myself into a young Chinese woman. I wore a pair of ripped jeans, a purple sweater and flat shoes. I had a backpack on my back with my camera hanging off my shoulder. I looked like a young tourist, perhaps an exchange student.

I pretended to take pictures of the city dock, but I was looking at Dash and Amilia sitting on the bench as their pups lay in a stroller. I continued to snap photos, getting closer to them. When I got closer, I heard them arguing.

“We are running out of money. We cannot live in the woods,” Amilia said to Dash.

“I’m doing the best that I can. We need to find a way to those Egyptian jewels. That store has maximum security, stronger than a damn bank,” Dash said.

“You shouldn’t have attacked them and maybe I would still been working there.”

“That was our deer. Those rich sons of bitches are sitting on goldmines. Xavier was too busy chasing after the jackal. He should’ve been chasing after the gold. I don’t want anymore of our wolves to get killed or kill one of theirs. All I want to do is support my pack then leave Goon and his pack alone."

When I walked past them, I could hear Dash sniffing. He looked at me then growled; I still smelled like Dayo.

"Who are you?" Dash asked me.

"A person that can help you," I said to him. Amilia growled then pulled the stroller closer to her.

"Help me how?" Dash asked me.

"I have some pieces of jewelry that are worth a lot of money, but of course, I need a favor from you."

"I don't do favors for strangers."

"Me neither, but desperate times calls for desperate measures." I went into my pocket pulling out a necklace that one of the Egyptian rulers wore centuries ago. "This could be worth a lot if you sell it to a historic museum, but of course, I need something from you," I said to Dash.

"What is it?" Amilia asked.

"Fall back. This is between the Alpha and I," I said, rolling my eyes at her.

I looked at Dash. "I want you to distract the other pack. Get any lone werewolf to join your pack. I need him and his pack ambushed by a lot of werewolves. They are strong, very strong, but they cannot defeat all of you," I said to him.

"What is the purpose?" Dash asked.

"They have something I want. All you have to do is get your clan together. I will know when you do. Once you are ready, I will find you."

Amilia looked at me. "I don't trust you. Why would a Chinese woman have a piece of ancient Egyptian jewelry?"

"The same reason why you have a piece of black dick and you are of a different ethnicity. I don't like to be questioned," I spat.

"Don't you talk to her like that. I will bite your damn throat out," he said to me.

"She's a witch," Amilia said out loud.

"You are worth more than just to breed with. You actually have a brain, but anyways, get the job done. There will be more pieces of jewelry where this came from," I said placing the necklace inside of his hand. I took a picture of his pups with my camera. Amilia jumped up.

"What did you do that for?" she asked me.

"Many spells can come about just by a picture. Do you think I would let you have a piece of jewelry knowing you might skip town? If you don't go through with my plan, these little pups will become a meal to a demon, and you know they like babies," I said to her. Amilia gasped and Dash looked at me with his pupils changing colors.

"Take this shit back. I will find another way," he said, shoving the necklace into me, causing me to fall.

"A deal is a deal. Once you touched that necklace, it was done. You walk away now, and you can kiss your pups good-bye. I will see you soon," I said then disappeared.

When I got back home, I smiled. I knew Dash was going to carry out his mission. Images of Dayo came into my head. I missed him. I craved him. I was going to get him back.

I sat down in the middle of the floor and closed my eyes to get an image of what Dayo was doing. I was able to see and hear his thoughts even with us being faraway because he marked a witch. When I saw a vision of him, he was on his motorcycle. When he stopped at a red light, he lifted up his helmet to eye a woman's behind as her hips seductively moved side to side.

"Come here for a second. Let me talk to you," he said to the busty black woman. She wasn't pretty, but she was very shapely. She looked to be only around twenty.

"The light is ready to turn green," the woman said back to him.

"I don't care about that, gorgeous. I would stop traffic for you any day," Dayo replied. The woman blushed then read off her number to him. He smiled at her then sped off when the light turned green. I looked up and down my house in search of my cell phone. I kept one because Adika said she wanted to be normal. That used to be our way of communicating. When I found it, I powered it on. It was ready to die out. I hurriedly dialed the number.

"Hello, this is Demoore," the woman answered sweetly.

"Stay the fuck away from him!" I screamed into the phone.

“Who is this?” she asked me with her music playing loudly in the background.

“This is his mate. Now, I have warned you. Take heed of my warning or else I will slit your throat while you sleep. I will sip on your soul like it’s fine fruity wine,” I said then the phone cut out. I wanted Dayo more than ever.

Dayo

"Bro, are you sure Kanya will let you out of the house?" I asked Goon. He looked at me then smirked.

"Don't make me body slam you, bro. The last time I did, Elle and Kofi had to snap your spine back in place," he said.

Izra walked into the den. He had been quiet lately since Adika lost their pup. Adika was cheerful, but Izra still moped around about it. Goon patted his shoulder then stuck something in his mouth covering his canines, top and bottom row. When he snapped them in, they were gold with diamonds. Izra finally smiled. "Ok, big bro. I see you," Izra said to Goon.

"Y'all muthafuckas been living it up without me, huh?" I asked them.

"We thought your gay ass was here," Izra spat, and then I growled at him.

"Don't tempt me, nigga. I would put your little ass on your back, lil bro. Goon, you better get this muthafucka," I said.

"Remember that time Goon body slammed you? He had you folded up like a cookout chair," Izra said laughing.

"This nigga watch too many rap videos," I said laughing Izra off. He was a pest.

Amadi and Elle walked into the living room, and Goon looked at their gear. "We are going to a strip club. We aren't going to work at Kanya's store," he told them. Elle and Amadi are the oldest, and they didn't really like to club. They had on casual wear for a professional crowd.

"I'm not leaving out of here dressed like a pup," Elle said.

"Nigga, you ain't got to dress like a pimp neither," I said to Elle, and then everyone cracked up laughing.

"I did miss your ass though. I don't like you, but I love you." Izra said to me; then I pushed him. Anik, Kanya, Adika and Jalesa came down the stairs dressed up. I would have to admit that the house seemed more alive since I've been back. Before Keora locked me away, it was just the pack brothers. The women brought more feeling to the mansion; it always seemed empty before.

“Where the fuck do you think you are going with that shit on?” Goon asked his mate.

“We are going to the club. The pups are with my mother and Arya. We are about to have fun too,” Kanya said.

“Change your clothes, Kanya,” Goon said. Kanya’s breasts were propped up in her form fitting dress, and her dress was a little too short.

“I told Adika this wasn’t going to work,” Kanya mumbled.

“You damn right it wasn’t going to work. Everyone else is covered up,” Goon spat. Kanya rolled her eyes then marched up the stairs growling and fussing.

Kanya’s mother walked into the den. “Don’t you all look young and vibrant, although you all are older than me,” she said. I wrapped my arm around her shoulder then whispered in her ear.

“I can make you feel young if you want me to. All you have to do is say the word,” I said to her.

"I'm a married woman, so you better watch it," she spat.

Kanya's father came downstairs. I thought maybe he would be going home, but there was a big blizzard in New York, and there wasn't any electricity.

"What's going on? What is the occasion?" he asked puffing on his cigar.

"I asked your wife if she would marry me," I said to him. Jeffrey charged into me, hitting me in the chest with his fist. He shook his hand.

"Damn it, what the hell do you have on under your shirt?" he asked me.

"He got a bulletproof vest on just in case we have a mob shootout," Izra said smirking with his arm around Adika's shoulder.

"You will leave my damn wife alone. Do you hear me? So help me God, I will kill you," Jeffery said.

I held my arms up. "No harm, sir. I was just playing," I told him.

Jeffery looked at Anik and Arya. "You two live here now too?" he asked them.

"Yes, Anik is my cousin, and she will be helping out at Beastly Pleasures. Is that okay with you?" Goon asked Jeffery.

"Who in the hell are these people? Every time I come up the stairs, I see new faces," he fussed.

"I don't live here, but I'm on my way out. I will see you all later," Jalesa said, walking to the door. Amadi walked out with her.

"What on earth is that in your mouth?" Jeffery asked, pushing his glasses up as he examined Goon's fangs.

"They're called grills," Goon answered. Kanya came back down the stairs with a longer dress and a crop jacket.

"What's the matter, daddy?" Kanya asked her father.

"This son of a bitch keeps hitting on my wife," he said.

"My mother is a bitch, sir—a female dog, might I add. I'm not offended at all," I said and everyone else chuckled.

"These people worship the devil. I need a damn drink." Jeffery said, storming off. Kanya looked at me, and I shrugged my shoulders.

*****

Few hours later…

I sat in our section sipping my cognac as I watched the crowd party on the dance floor. I was actually quite bored. I use to live for the wild partying human life. I just wanted to hunt then go to sleep. Everyone else was partying, but I was bored. Anik came and sat down next to me. She has been staying with us for about four days now. She was quiet and didn't say much.

"What's the matter? Everyone else is celebrating your homecoming," she said to me. Anik was gorgeous, her voice sultry and smooth. I bet she could sing if she wanted to. The way she moves is even smooth and alluring.

"I'm bored," I said to her.

"You are a young wolf. Where is your spunk?" she asked me.

"You're young yourself. I'm surprised you have a grown pup."

"Arya isn't really my daughter. I fell in love with her father. Her father was raising her since her mother was raped and killed by a group of lone wolves. I love her like she is my own, but I'm not old enough to go into heat yet. So, I guess you could say I'm young also."

"You are such an asshole!" I heard a voice shout from behind me. When I turned around, Demoore's face was scrounged up in anger.

"Pardon me," I said to her.

"A woman called my phone threatening to kill me. I guess it's that bitch that is sitting next to you. You told me you wasn't seeing anyone."

Anik slid away from me then joined Kanya and Adika on the dance floor. My pack brothers eyed me with smirks on their faces. I was always known for getting into shit, but human women have recently become an addiction.

"I don't know what you are talking about, but you are more than welcome to have a drink with me," I said, grabbing her hand then kissing it. Her mood changed, and she sat down next to me.

Bro, I have seen raccoons with rabies look better than that, Goon's voice boomed in my head.

Did you see the ass though, bro? I responded, and then he shook his head.

Kanya is synced into my thoughts; I wouldn't dare look. I think Anik likes you. She's been staring at you all night."

Anik isn't my type, bro. Her scent is alluring, but I rather fuck a human than my own kind. I'm not trying to mark someone; I'm not ready for anyone's pups."

I excused myself then went to the bathroom. The men's bathroom was empty. After I finished handling my business, I washed my hands. When I pulled on the door, it was locked.

"What the fuck!" I shouted, trying to pull on the door, but it wouldn't open. I heard a laugh, and it was a familiar laugh.

"My sweet Dayo," a voice said inside one of the stalls. When the door opened, a Chinese woman stepped out.

"Cut the shit, Keora." She turned back into herself and was standing in front of me with an all-black, see-through outfit on. Her nipples were pointy and erect. A low growl escaped from my throat. I wanted to kill her, but I couldn't.

She had some type of hold on me. It was all because she tricked me into marking her. She disappeared then reappeared in my face with her arms wrapped around me. Her long locks framed her pretty face. The weird piercings in her cheek made her look even more unique. Maybe this is why I was bored with my life. I felt like I belonged someplace else. Being with her would mean I would have to betray my pack, and brotherhood always came first. I grabbed her by the neck, choking her. "I should kill you," I gritted, slamming her against the wall.

"You couldn't if you wanted to," she taunted me. My fangs grew out, and then I bit her as hard as I could. With my other hand, I unbuckled my belt then dropped my pants. I released my hardened dick. When I pulled away from her, blood dripped from her neck then disappeared. I slid the thin material that she wore up to her hips then entered her. Her long witch nails scratched my neck as I roughly thrust inside of her. Her pussy squeezed me; she was soaking wet. I licked her neck then bit her nipple through the material she was wearing. I then gently sucked on it. Keora's legs wrapped around me. I pressed into her body, and her back was firmly against the wall as I stuffed my dick inside of her. Sweet-like whimpers slipped from her lips. She was no longer the bitch that had been wreaking havoc on our lives. She was someone else; she was the real her. I felt a burst of energy travel throughout my body. I grinded into her spot over and over again, causing her to scream. I lifted her legs over the crook of my arms, slamming her down onto my dick as I stretched her open.

"I miss you so much," she moaned, licking my lips. My dick swelled, and Keora gasped when she felt the pressure from my size and width penetrating her tight walls. I howled when I released inside of her. After I was done, I pulled out of her, dropping her onto the floor. I was ashamed that I was feeling something for an evil witch.

"I'm sorry, Dayo," she said. Then just like that, she was gone. I fixed myself then pulled on the door. When I went back to our section, everyone was looking at me.

"You couldn't wait until you got home to take a dump? You been gone for a while," Izra said, slurring as he lay in Adika's lap smoking a blunt. Everyone was drinking and smoking, but I wanted to be alone. Demoore rubbed my back then kissed my cheek.

"Do you want to get out of here?" she asked me. Anik looked at Demoore then rolled her eyes.

He must like whores, Anik said when I heard her thoughts. I tried to think of everything except Keora. I didn't want anyone to hear my thoughts. When I was around them, my thoughts were elsewhere.

"Not tonight. I'm not in the mood," I said to Demoore. She sucked her teeth then stood up to join the crowd that danced wildly on the dance floor.

"You sure you aren't gay? I have never seen you turn down pussy? Are you okay, bro?" Izra asked me.

"One more word, Izra, and I will come over there to fuck you up. Matter of fact, I'm done with this shit." I stood up then walked out the club. I got on my motorcycle then sped home, weaving in and out of lanes until I got back to the mansion.

I woke up before sunrise to go hunting. When I was in the woods I smelled a familiar scent. When I followed the trail, I came across Anik. She was crouched down with her head bowed down over the small deer she had killed. After a few seconds, she tore into the baby deer. Chippewa wolves were different from what I had learned. They were more about nature, and they hated to kill. Before they ate their kill, they would bow their heads down asking for forgiveness. She turned then looked at me. She huffed then continued to eat. Her wolf had a round, red dot in the middle of her forehead. The tips of Anik's paws were red and so was the ring around her tail. I had never really paid attention to her. I sat and watched her eat. Was it possible to have a desire for a wolf like myself?

After she was done eating, she walked past me. Her long, bushy tail dragged along the ground. Blood covered her feminine, small face. I licked her face. It wasn't a sexual gesture; it was like offering a human a napkin if she had something on her face.

Thank you, her voice spoke inside of my head. Anik tried to walk away, but I playfully nudged her with my head. Her smaller body rolled on the ground. Anik reminded me of a younger sister, but there was something about her aura. She was a mystery to me. Most wolves are aggressive. Anik didn't have an ounce of that in her. She was too perfect. She playfully bit my neck then growled. I rolled over on her, and then she kicked me with her hind legs then took off running. I chased behind her; she was fast. When I caught up to her, I gently bit her. Goon and Kanya jumped out of the bushes followed by some type of cat.

I hate fucking cats! I shouted.

It's me, Adika.

Izra, is fucking a feline? What type of bestiality is that? I asked her, and she hissed at me. Goon smelled a deer, and his big black wolf took off in its direction. Kanya and Adika ran behind him. I smelled them too. There were four deer close by and one big buck. I wasn't really hungry. I chose to hunt later.

Anik lay out in the shade chewing on a thick piece of wood to get the chunks of flesh she had between her teeth. Once she was done, she shifted into her human form with her back turned towards me. She had red paintings around her hips. I eyed her plump bottom and her thick, juicy legs.

She grabbed her clothes, went behind a tree then put them on. I shifted back to human form. When she turned around, she gasped.

"You never seen a dick before?" I asked her.

"I was going to save myself until I went in heat. My mate never showed me himself in that manner," she said, eyeing my piece.

"Are you a virgin?" I asked her.

"Yes, I am. I guess that really turned you off. I will see you later. I need to get dressed. Today will be the first day I work in a real place," she said then scurried off.

"Stay away from her." Keora was speaking to me inside of my head again.

"Go to hell and leave me the fuck alone. If we wasn't concerned about Adika, you would've been dead by now", I thought. She didn't respond. I needed to tell the pack, but I didn't know how to tell them. She cursed me, making me feel things for her I shouldn't. Was I betraying my pack?

Naobi

I walked to the end of the temple with a hooded cape over my head. Ammon was asleep when I snuck out of our bed. A woman wasn't supposed to roam around alone at night in Anubi. Out of the darkness at the end of the hall, Jalesa stepped out.

She bowed her head down to me.

"What did you find? Did you see Saka?" I asked her.

"No, I haven't seen him or felt his presence around Keora's sanctuary. I think her heart is getting pure; she is in love. If she is in love, then Saka would no longer have someone to use as a puppet. His time as a spirit is running out. I put an invisible shield around Goon's house. No outsiders will be able to get to the pack or the pups," Jalesa said.

"Keora needs to be put away in an immortal prison for eternity, but it will take a very strong spell to put her there. It isn't easy putting a demon witch inside of a prison. We need to hurry. Your spell is going to wear off soon, and you won't be able to come back and forth between earth and Anubi."

As I spoke to Jalesa, A warrior marched down the hall with a fire torch. I pulled Jalesa into a small room until he passed us. After he went down the other end, I whispered, "Demon witches feed off anything to become powerful. Whatever you do, stay away from her until you know she is easy to capture." Jalesa nodded her head in response.

I smiled at Jalesa, but my smile quickly faded. "Your time on earth is limited. Do not hurt yourself by falling in love because it isn't going anywhere," I said to her. She put her head down.

"I know, but Amadi has a heart of the finest gold. Our first date was amazing. He gave me flowers then fed me fresh fruit. He even massaged my feet. For the first time, I felt like royalty. I need to tell him that soon before I no longer exist to him," she said.

"NAOBI!" Ammon's deep voice roared throughout the halls. Jalesa disappeared. He wasn't happy that I had left our bed. I stepped out into the light of the fire torches that decorated the aged stone walls.

"Yes, Ammon," I answered him.

"What are you doing roaming around the temple this late at night?" he asked me. He crossed his strong arms over his broad chest and looked down at me like a child misbehaving. His eyes turned blue; his beast was angry with me.

"I had a vision," I said, walking away from him.

He grabbed me by the arm, lifting me up off the floor. "Are you meddling in Akua's life again?" he roared.

"No, now put me down," I said to him. He snapped his fingers, and then five warriors came running down the hall with spears and shields.

"What are you doing?" I asked him.

Ammon threw some dust on me that made me weak. It was a punishment for witches who misbehaved.

He held up my secret spell book, the one I used to send Jalesa back and forth to Anubi and earth.

"This is what you have been busy with while neglecting you duties as my mate? You have been over stepping your boundaries. Akua is the son of Ammon. He has the heart of a warrior. You shame me when you try to fight his battles. Is my blood that runs through his veins not good enough?" Ammon yelled, causing the temple to shake.

"Why are you doing this?" I cried.

"Akua will fight his battles like a warrior! He will not have his mother interfere with centuries of tradition. His wolf will lead him through whatever problems he has to face, and he will defeat it. He will be who he was made to be."

"You will regret this," I seethed as the warriors picked me up.

"Take her to the tower. She will be locked away until she learns how to be a mate. It's over Naobi," he said to me as they carried me away. He looked at me with sadness in his eyes. He didn't want to do what he was doing to me.

They put me in the tower then locked the gate. "When I get out of here, I will turn all of you into beetles then step on you!" I screamed. Ammon is king, and his orders overpower mine.

"Oh no, Jalesa will be stuck on earth," I said to myself. I had to warn someone, but I couldn't. I was in an immortal prison.

"Ammon, I will never bed with you again! Do you hear me! Find another mate because I'm going to kill you when I get out." I screamed loud enough so he could hear me. I flopped down on the prison floor. I needed to find a way out. I closed my eyes then concentrated on widening the rails.

"ARRGGHHHHHHHHHHH!" I screamed as my head pounded. The rails widened a little, but it weakened me. I fell down onto the floor then lay there. It was going to take a while, but I was determined, even if it weakened me.

Baki, one of the younger warriors, came to the rails. "This is an immortal prison. How did you do that?" he asked with fear in his eyes.

"I am Naobi. I created all of this. If it wasn't for Ammon getting bit by a wolf, my curse upon werewolves would've never existed. Now, you can either let me out, or I can sit here and break out," I said to him.

“Ammon would not approve,” he said. I reached my hand out in a squeezing gesture, and Baki fell down, grabbing his neck. Two warriors ran to him.

“This prison is supposed to make immortals like humans,” one of them said.

I squeezed my hand tighter until blood dripped onto the floor. Baki’s eyes rolled to the back of his head then turned red. I was getting weaker as I forced my powers, but I wouldn’t let them see it.

“Stop it!” one of the warriors screamed.

“Get me out of here, or all of you are next,” I said as Baki struggled to breathe. I didn’t want to kill him, but I wanted to frighten them. They pulled out the weird shaped key—a key I made many ages ago. The warrior put it into the lock, and then it opened. When I walked out, I collapsed…

*****

I woke up and looked around. I was in a different room. I hurriedly sat up. "Be easy, my queen," a familiar voice said.

"Ammon hurt me," I said to Kofi. He wiped my forehead with a wet rag.

"Ammon needs to give more attention to his mate. He is ready to have another pup," Kofi said to me.

"I don't have the desire," I said, sitting up and stuffing grapes inside of my mouth from the tray that lay beside me. Opal walked into the small room; she's Kofi's mate. Her hair was braided down to her hips with gold and blue beads at the end. Her gold silk robe clung to her figure. Kanya looked identical to her ancestor. Opal was born a thousand years ago with jackal blood, the same blood as Kanya. Opal bowed her head down to me. "Morning, my queen," she said. I reached my hand out to her, and she took my hand then pulled me up.

"I told Ammon that not even immortal prisons can stop you," Opal said to me.

"Where is he?"

"He went out hunting. He has been gone for a while," Kofi said.

"I'm going to curse him," I spat. Then they laughed.

"You have done so millions of times. You know when I see you and Ammon, It reminds me of Goon and Kanya," Kofi laughed.

"I want to meet Kanya," Opal said.

"She is just like you. She even looks a lot like you. I've heard that she can be a little feisty," I told Opal.

"Your bath is ready, my queen," Kaira said to me. She was a servant. I wasn't too fond of her, and nor was she fond of me. Opal left the room with Kofi following behind her.

Kaira shut the door and poured water into the small hole on the floor that served as a tub. "When will I be allowed to tell Kofi about our son?" she asked me.

"You seduced a mated male. You are lucky you didn't get punished," I told her as I undressed.

"He doesn't even know I was with child!" Kaira shouted with her eyes changing; she is a werewolf. She seduced many wolves, all who had a mate. Some wolves could resist, but Kofi couldn't. Opal was raped by a gang of wolves many ages ago. Her scent was like Kanya's. Her scent previously turned many wolves into lusting beasts. Kofi was turned off by Opal's scent after the incident, and he turned to Kaira who was in heat.

"Pups that are born to wolves that are not soul mates cannot live in Anubi. You mated with a wolf who had a mate, which is not acceptable! You want to be a Jezebel, then go on earth to do that with some of the humans who don't take traditions seriously!" I shouted at her.

"I just want to see my pup."

"Dash is fine. He even has two pups now. He is the Alpha of his pack. Just be thankful that shifters raised him as their own on earth," I said to her as I stepped into the water.

"You evil witch!" she screamed.

"If I were evil, I would tell Opal what you did. Opal has a mean bite."

Kaira was ready to yell at me, but before she could, I snapped my fingers, and her lips sealed shut. I laughed as I relaxed in the tub.

"I can't hear you or your thoughts. Now get out!" I said to her. She headed to the door, and then I turned around. "Stay away from my mate. I can see that you are in heat again," I said to her but she couldn't respond.

After my bath, I got dressed then went into my hidden room. I looked at my crystal-like globe that not even Ammon knew about. I wanted to see what I have been neglecting to see. It was my extra pair of eyes. I could see Akua's and his pack. I could even see Ammon running through the grass field while chasing a gazelle. Kaira was standing there watching him, and he sniffed the air because of her scent. I could hear his thoughts; he was aroused by her. She was tempting him, but he walked away. Ammon had thoughts about bedding Kaira. While I was watching our son, Kaira has been watching my mate.

*****

We all sat down at the long table awaiting our feast. The servants came into the feasting area to pour us wine. I watched Ammon. No words have been exchanged since he locked me away. Kaira poured wine into his cup. I watched her gestures. Her scent was tempting him; I could see it in his eyes. Werewolves are loyal to their mates, but even they get temptations when they aren't getting pleasure. Werewolves are very sexual beasts. When Kaira walked away, Ammon's eyes turned because of how badly he wanted her. Everyone sat down and ate, drinking wine as Egyptian music played.

Thousands and thousands of years ago, you and I became one. I have never seen you look at another wolf with pleasure," I said to his thoughts. He sipped his wine.

Thousands and thousands of years, you never neglected your duties as my mate, Ammon replied back.

I pushed myself away from the table then walked past him. He followed behind me into our room.

"I'm lonely, Naobi," he said to me while my back was turned towards him.

Tears fell from my eyes. "I can't have any more pups. Akua almost killed me when I had him. Not even the strongest witch can give birth to a werewolf. I begged my father, Saka, to give me strength so I could have Akua. I promised him that I would give him Akua's soul after a few years. He said Akua's soul would make him stronger. I created Adika and Keora to watch over Akua so I could come up with a curse to put Saka away so he wouldn't take Akua from us," I said to Ammon.

Ammon threw my spell book at me then walked out of the room.

"How much longer do I have to wait for you, Naobi? I need to hold you. I want to feel the inside of you. My dreams of you are just dreams. I need it to be reality," the voice said.

"Your wish will be granted soon", I said to him with a tear falling from my eye.

Goon

Kanya and I were walking through the mall as Kanya pushed the double seated stroller with the pups in them.

"Look at these outfits, Goon. Wouldn't the twins look adorable in them?" Kanya asked me. I shook my head. I had almost ten bags in my hands because Kanya liked shopping.

"Can we leave? Damn," I said.

"Give me five more minutes, baby. Let me run in here for one second," she said, pushing the twins into the store.

"Mr. Prince," I heard a voice come from behind me. When I turned around, it was Dash and two new wolves that might've joined his pack.

"I see you had to replace the slaughtered ones," I chuckled as they growled. The two new wolves that stood beside him looked to be young; they were rebels. Young wolves kill just for the fun. Some of them even kill humans too just for the taste of blood. They were both dressed in hoodies with sagging pants. The one with the cornrows grilled me then growled. “Who is this lame, Dash?” The dark-skinned one asked.

I looked at Dash and noticed he had on expensive clothes. “You found a job I see.” Dash started to sweat, and the vein in his neck popped out; he wanted to shift. Kanya came out of the store. “That sexy bitch belongs to you?” The loudmouthed wolf with the cornrows said to me.

“Kanya, take the twins to the car,” I told her. She didn’t want to leave me, but we had our pups. She grabbed all of the bags I had in my hands then stormed off, pushing the stroller. If she was human, she wouldn’t have been able to do that.

“Damn, and she got a fat ass,” The one with the cornrows said, grabbing his dick. I punched him in the face causing his body to fly into the glass window of the store’s showcase. I jumped into the window. He tried to get up, but I hit him again. People screamed as his body flew into a cash register.

"Run that shit by me again, muthafucka!" I said, punching him again. His body started to shift; young wolves couldn't control when they shifted. One lady fainted after the young wolf's ears grew out, and his teeth sharpened. His face grew into a snout, and then he growled.

"It's a wolf!" someone screamed. I used my mind as I concentrated; everyone in the mall froze. The wolf charged into me while I was in human form. Dash and the other wolf tried to all attack me at once. All three of them were in wolf form. I shifted then started to attack them as they jumped on me. We knocked over a few people who were still frozen. All three of them bit me viciously. I shook them off of me then attacked Dash since he was close to me. I sank my teeth into his neck as he bit my face. Dash and I rolled out of the store and into a bench. One man was stuck with his melted ice cream cone in his hand. The other two wolves bit my hind legs to slow me down, but it only made me more aggressive. I slammed Dash then knocked the two of the other wolves over, biting the both of them. The one who had the cornrows charged into me. I caught him by the neck then crawled up the wall with him inside of my mouth. I burst through the ceiling window then leaped into the parking lot. Cars slammed on breaks, and people started running until they froze in place. When they come to, they won't remember anything that they had seen. Our identity is to remain a secret; humans couldn't know we existed among them.

I snapped the young wolf's neck then bit into it. I shook him by the neck until his neck was mangled with his head slightly attached. I dragged the dead wolf body into the nearest woods and waited for Dash and the other wolf to find me.

Are you okay? Where are you? Kanya's voice panicked inside of my head.

In the woods by the mall. Get my pups home like I told you!" I shouted.

You want me to leave you? Kanya asked me.

Go the fuck home, Kanya, before I get madder!" my voice boomed. I put the dead wolf up in a tree then leapt from tree to tree and waited for a few moments. Dash and the other wolf ran into the woods sniffing.

Do you think the other wolves are following his mate? Didn't Keora say to distract them so she could get to whatever it is that she wanted? the young wolf said into Dash's head.

Shut the fuck up! He might be near, and he can hear your thoughts dumb-ass, Dash said into the young wolf's thoughts.

Goon, I'm being followed by a big group of wolves while I have the twins in the truck. We were set up, Kanya said.

I left Dash and the young wolf roaming around in the woods. I took off towards my home, running as fast as I could.

When I got to the house, about fifteen wolves had Kanya surrounded by the gate. Dayo, Amadi, Elle, Izra, Adika and Anik were all leaping over the gate to attack. I charged into the wolves, biting any wolf that was close to me. I needed to get to my pups. Kanya shifted then burst out of the window with the twins in her mouth, clinging to them by their clothes. They screamed and cried as she leapt over the gate then took off towards the house. The wolves tried to leap over the fence, but a force was turning them to ashes. Our house was shielded; they couldn't get over the gate. Three wolves were left alive after we viciously attacked the other wolves, killing them like flies. The three wolves took off running, and the pack and I chased them. When we caught up to them, we ripped them apart. Dayo, Elle and I pulled a wolf apart as it howled, our teeth piercing through its flesh. Blood dripped from our mouths as we howled. Our deep howls could be heard miles away; we were warning the other pack that it was war.

Moments later, everyone in the pack sat around me. I was glad that Kanya's parents left to go home before the wolves came to our house.

"What the hell was that?" Anik asked.

"We were distracted so that Keora could take Akea, but her plan didn't work. This pack is stronger than twenty wolves together. We are bigger and we are stronger," I said, pacing back and forth. Kanya held onto the twins shaking. Her teeth had put wounds on them. I had to give them my blood for their wounds to close up. My blood boiled. "When we go onto their territory, we will kill anything in sight! Even if they surrender, we still kill! Fuck pack rules. They are dead!" I growled.

I kneeled down in front of Kanya and moved the hair out of her face. "You were only trying to protect them," I told her. She squeezed the twins closer to her.

"I almost killed them," she said.

"It's in our nature to grab our pups with our mouths," I told her. The pack was in an uproar as I tried to calm Kanya down.

"Why is this happening to us?" Kanya asked me.

"We discussed this after we found Dayo; Saka wants Akea,"

"He isn't getting our damn baby. Where can we find him?"

"Only Keora knows. Don't worry. We will find her. I bet Dayo knows where she's at."

Dayo stood up. "What the fuck does that mean?" he asked me.

"You marked her didn't you? She pops up in your head doesn't she?" I asked Dayo. We went to Keora's house a few times after we found Adika and Dayo. Keora could sense when we were coming.

"No, she doesn't," Dayo said.

"She knew where we were going to be. I would've known if Kanya and I were being followed. I told you where we were going before we left, and she heard me through your visions. She can see and hear what we do through your fucking visions. She is probably hearing us now," I said to him.

Everyone looked at Dayo, and Anik growled at him. I noticed over the past few weeks that they have been getting close.

"Come on, bro. Don't tell us you still fucking the witch," Elle said to Dayo. Dayo sat with his head down. "Muthafucka, I should kick your ass! You mean to tell me you are still fucking that bitch, and you couldn't kill her?" Izra said charging into Dayo. Elle and Amadi pulled them apart.

"I can't! I feel a connection to her. I can't help what she did to me. The bitch cursed me! I get urges for her," Dayo shouted.

Anik grabbed Arya's hand then walked out of the room.

"Anik!" Dayo called out to her, but she didn't answer.

"As bad as I want to rip your fucking throat out, I can't. If you marked her, it's only natural that you feel this way about her," I said to Dayo.

"We have to keep you out of our plans," Elle said to Dayo.

"WHAT! I'm still a part of this pack," Dayo fussed.

"You will always be our brother, but Goon said Keora can see us through you. That means she knows all our plans that we discussed as a pack. She knows everything, bro. She is using you to get an inside look into our lives," Amadi told Dayo.

"Goon, I told you what you should do to me," Adika said.

"Would you shut the fuck up? Nobody is going to kill you. Damn, you say stupid shit when you get mad," Izra yelled at Adika.

"Adika, please don't say that. I need you right now. There has to be another way to get rid of Keora," Kanya said.

"What other way? An immortal prison would keep her and strip her from all of her powers. Naobi is the only witch that can put her there, but Naobi cannot stay on earth long enough to do that. Goon can do it, but he doesn't practice spells or curses," Adika said.

The next day, Kanya stayed home, and Anik went to the Beastly Treasures to keep the business going. Kanya said that Anik's down-to-earth personality and aura drew in more costumers. I cut up pieces of raw meat to take to Kanya. When I walked into our bedroom, she was packing her clothes and the twins' clothes.

"What are you doing?" I asked her.

"I'm going to stay with my parents for a while. I feel like the pups cannot be protected here," she said to me. I never showed real aggression towards Kanya, but at that moment, I wanted to attack her.

I snatched the suitcases away from her then tossed them across the room; her clothes flew all over the place.

"I'm tired of this shit with you!" I yelled at her. My body temperature rose. I wanted to attack her. I was ready to forget that she was my mate, and she gave me pups.

"I'm scared. There is an evil warlock preying on my damn baby!" Kanya said.

Adika came into our room then grabbed the pups out of their cribs. I guess she knew that Kanya and I were about to shift. Adika called for my pack brothers to come and get me before things got out of hand.

"You can go, but leave my pups here. They are safer here than at your human parents' house. If a wolf gets a hold of them, they are dead! You would put them and our pups in jeopardy!" I yelled at her.

"You can't protect us neither, so what fucking difference does that make?"

"That's how you feel about me? If so, then you can get the fuck out and leave my pups here, bitch," I seethed with my fangs withdrawing from my mouth. Black hairs pricked through my skin. I was ready to shift, but I couldn't. If I did, Kanya wasn't going to be safe around me. She seemed to be against me. In our beast nature, we targeted anything and anyone who seemed to be an opponent. Kanya's beast looked at me like an opponent as well. Even if she didn't want to attack me, she couldn't control it. She shifted then charged into me, but I had already turned into a wolf. Her canines pierced through my neck, and I bit her shoulder then slammed her into a wall. She charged back, clawing into my face. Kanya is the only one who could possibly kill me. I wouldn't heal as fast as I usually did.

She sank her teeth into my neck, locking her jaw. I bit her as hard as I could. I could feel the pain I was causing her, but her beast wanted to kill me. In the animal kingdom, real wolves and jackals fought. They are natural born enemies. But in our tribe, she is my soul mate. I avoided biting her neck. My jaw was stronger than hers. If I bit her neck hard enough, I could snap it and kill her. I wouldn't be able to live with myself if I did that.

The other wolves charged into our room, pulling us apart and bum-rushing us. Izra pulled me by my hind leg with his teeth piercing through my leg. I howled out in pain. It looked like Kanya and I were being attacked, but we weren't. I felt blood dripping from my neck onto the floor. I loved Kanya so much that I was willing to let her kill me because I couldn't bare killing her. Since I met Kanya, I have been able to control my beast. If I didn't control him, Kanya would've been dead. Kanya's jackal neck isn't as strong as a wolf. Even though she is part of me, I would've killed her in seconds.

I lay down on the floor panting, losing my blood. Anik put pressure on my neck with her paw. Izra shifted into human form.

"Kanya, what did you do?" he yelled at her. Kanya backed away into the corner as the pack growled at her. I howled at them to leave her alone. I tried to get up to protect her, but I was weak. It was in my pack's nature to protect me; that was the reason they were bred.

Everyone shifted back except Kanya. She walked out of the room with Anik following behind her. My eyes closed, and my body slowly started to shift back to human form. My brothers picked me up then laid me down on the bed.

“He is losing a lot of blood, Elle!” Izra yelled. My body got weak. I yelled out in pain when I tried to heal myself. I was too weak for my wounds to close on their own like they usually did. Amadi ran out of the room then came back in.

“This is about to burn, bro,” he said, pouring some type of liquid onto my neck.

“ARRRRRGGHHHHHHHHHH!” I shouted. Kanya stood in the doorway with a robe on. She ran to me then hugged me.

“I’m so sorry. I couldn’t control it,” she cried, holding onto me. Izra and Dayo pulled her off me.

“Get your ass back! You almost killed him,” Dayo said to her. Dayo pulled Kanya out of the room, and she screamed, kicked and cried.

“Bro, I don’t give a fuck who she is to you. I almost snapped her neck. You let her get away with too much shit. She doesn’t appreciate shit you do for her. You got her a store, and she is barely there. You cater to her, and look what she does to you; she almost killed you,” Izra said to me.

Elle and Amadi wrapped my neck up. It was starting to close up. That was the first time I experienced real pain before healing. My pack brothers cleaned up the room. Kanya and I had things everywhere. It looked like we had an earthquake. There were even holes and cracks in the walls.

When I went downstairs, everyone was silent. Arya watched cartoons eating raw meat chunks. Adika had the twins rocking back in forth in their swing. I went into the kitchen and walked straight into an argument between Dayo and Anik.

"What the fuck do you want from me, Anik? You and I are like brother and sister? I don't understand your attitude!" Dayo yelled at her.

"It doesn't matter. I'm saving up my money that Kanya is giving me from working at her store. I appreciate you all letting me and Arya come here because we didn't have a place to go. I am very thankful that Goon let us in without knowing us, but this isn't working for me," Anik said with her head down.

"Today has been a rough day, and you are talking out of your head. It isn't safe for a female wolf to be alone with a pup. Some wolf gangs rape females then kill their pups," Dayo said to her.

"We've been doing just fine," Anik said, walking out of the kitchen.

Dayo looked at me. "Good to see you up, bro," he said patting my shoulder.

"It feels good to be up. I still can't believe my mate tried to kill me. I didn't know who she was."

"She was you, bro. She can't control herself just like you couldn't ages ago. She is still learning, but she feels fucked up about it. She locked herself in the room in the basement. Elle and Amadi tried to get her to come out, but she didn't. They said all they heard was her crying. I almost feel bad for her," Dayo said.

"Kanya and I need to be away from each other for a few days. My beast is very vengeful."

"I should've told y'all about Keora. That night at the club, she locked me inside of the bathroom. I fucked her. I didn't want to, but she got a hold on me. She pops up in my head. She taunts me in my dreams. The crazy witch even threatened me to stay away from Anik. I got a feeling she will try to hurt her. Anik is too special for something to happen to her."

"She is acting like a scorned human woman," I chuckled then got serious. "We will fix it, but Anik is acting like that because she is ready to go into heat. She will become very jealous, maybe aggressive. She is a young female; Kanya showed the same signs as her," I told Dayo. I went into the fridge to grab the pup's bottles. I warmed them up then headed to the living room.

"Uncle Goon, can I help you feed them?" Arya said to me.

"Come over here and feed Kanye. But you got to keep still; you are too hyper," I told her. Arya sat down next to me, and I gave her Kanye. She smiled. "I want a pup," Arya said.

"Anik, get your ass in here and talk to Arya. I'm not having this conversation with her. It's too many damn females in here," I mumbled. After I fed the pups then changed them, I headed out into the woods. I needed to learn the other side of me, and I needed to have a clear head.

I heard bushes moving. I turned around and it was Jalesa.

"What do you want?" I asked her. She handed me a spell book.

"Naobi wanted me to give this to you. The spells are written in an ancient handwriting. You will be able to read it once you open the book; it's in your blood," Jalesa said then disappeared.

"Damn, she is weird," I said out loud.

Kanya

"You don't look too good," I said to Anik after she waited on a costumer. Anik was sweating, and her skin looked clammy. She sat down in the leather chair behind the showcase.

"I feel a sensation between my legs, and every time I see Dayo, I feel bubbly," she said.

"Are you leaking between your legs?" I asked her.

"Yes," she said, feeling embarrassed.

"You are ready to mate. Your body wants to carry a pup."

"I can't do that! I need to take care of Arya."

"I know that feeling. I felt the same way when Goon told me I needed to mate. But I was already connected to him. I felt it when I first saw him. How could I try to kill him, Anik? I don't like what I have become. This is the part I hate about being an animal." Anik touched my hand then smiled at me, and just like that, my heart warmed. I haven't known her long, but I felt like I have known her as long as I've known Adika.

"Goon knows you didn't mean it. I have never seen a beast that didn't act like one. In nature, we are wild but loving animals. It's a gift. Just have more faith in Goon. Appreciate him, and then it will all come into play," she said.

"I only come upstairs when he hunts. Then when he comes back, I go back down to my room. I'm even thinking about going to live with my parents. Maybe the twins are better off with their father."

Anik went into her black blazer pocket then pulled out a pretty orange stone with blue swirls in it.

"This is beautiful," I said to her.

"Before my family was slaughtered, my mother gave this to me. She said it made her feel at peace. I think you need it more than I do."

"I can't take this. It's special to you."

"Now it can be special to you," she said to me. I put the pretty stone inside of my blazer pocket.

"Were you in love with your mate?" I asked Anik.

"Arya's father's tribe had more money than my family. My family was poor. We had to eat the scraps left over from the other wolves. My parents thought I would be better off with an older wolf. He had a young baby and needed help. I helped him and he gave my family money in return. It was an arrangement, and he never touched me. I honestly think he just needed me there for his daughter. A gang of wolves came into our small, hidden town and wiped the rest of us out. Arya and I have been homeless, migrating from state to state ever since. I'm very thankful you let me work here."

"I don't want you and Arya to leave. The mansion is big enough for all of us. Plus, Arya likes to help Amadi make his oils," I said to her. Dayo, Amadi and Izra walked into the store. "What's going on?" I asked them. Amadi only comes to deliver his oils that we give out in the jewelry bags as free gifts.

"We just came here to make sure y'all was straight," Izra said.

"Are the twins with their father?" I asked them.

"Naw, Elle got them. Goon is studying some spell shit," Dayo said, eyeing Anik. Anik hurriedly went to the back. "Is it just me, or did Anik's ass get fatter and her breasts rounder?" Dayo asked.

"As much as I want to look, I can't. Adika will fuck my ass up. Y'all know she made my dick disappear," Izra said.

"It's disrespectful to voice a woman's bodily appearance out loud," Amadi said.

"Can someone tell the gods to come and get this old, ancient-ass nigga?" Dayo asked, making Izra laugh.

Amadi pushed Dayo. "Don't fuck with me, bro. I might be a little behind in the times, but my ass whippings aren't."

A man walked in. He looked to be around twenty-five. Anik came out because the staff was assisting other customers.

"Welcome to Beastly Treasures. How may I assist you today," Anik asked the guy. The guy was brown-skinned and kind of short. He wasn't all that attractive, but he had a pretty smile.

"I thought this jewelry was beautiful, but I have to take that back. You are more stunning," The stranger said to Anik, causing her to blush.

"Bro, did she just blush at that muthafucka? Look at his tight-ass suit," Dayo said.

I rolled my eyes at him. "Well at least he has good taste in women," I said to Dayo.

Izra and Amadi went to the back to stock the oils while Dayo stood watching Anik interact with the stranger. I could tell Dayo secretly liked Anik, but he didn't want to show it.

"What's the matter, Dayo?" I asked him. He looked at me then growled.

"Shut the hell up, and you better not tell Goon I said that shit to you. He practicing that voodoo shit now," Dayo said to me.

"I saw this outfit at the mall the other day. I think it would look good on Anik for her date that he is going to ask her on. All she needs me to do is her make-up," I teased Dayo.

"I don't like you," Dayo said to me then smirked.

“I don’t like you neither, brother.”

After Anik exchanged numbers with the stranger, she assisted him with looking for a necklace for his grandmother’s birthday. After he purchased the necklace, he kissed Anik’s hand then left out of the store.

“What was he talking about?” Dayo asked Anik.

Don’t tell him! It’s not his business, and I have an outfit in mind for your date. As soon as we close up, we can hit the mall, I said into her thoughts. Anik looked at me then smiled, but Dayo didn’t look too pleased.

After we closed down the store, my pack brothers followed us out. They even escorted us to the mall. Dayo didn’t say much to Anik. He seemed bothered by something as he kept looking around. When we got to the parking lot, Keora was standing by our big SUV.

“Isn’t this cute,” Keora said. She wasn’t disguised this time; she was as herself. I have only seen her as herself once, and that was when she saved me after I was attacked by Xavier and Aki. I growled at her.

“There are humans out here,” Amadi whispered to me.

"I told you to stay away from her, didn't I?" Keora asked Dayo.

"Calm down, Kanya. If you kill her, then Adika dies too. She will get her day. She knows wolves aren't allowed to shift around humans. She's only trying to taunt us," Amadi whispered to me.

Keora leaned against our truck, looking at her long witch nails. She was dressed in black pants, a black leather jacket and black pumps. Her locks hung down loosely reaching her small hips. She blew Dayo a kiss.

"My Dayo isn't happy to see me? We had many memorable nights, didn't we?" she asked him.

"Why are you fucking with me?" Dayo asked her. Keora looked into his eyes, and I could see the love she had for him.

"I want you to come back. If you do, I will call Dash's pack off."

"Dash's pack is the least of our worries. This bitch isn't all that smart is she, Dayo?" Izra asked him.

Keora looked at us. "I will be waiting," she laughed then disappeared.

"Remind me to never fuck Adika over again because if heartbroken witches act like this, then I don't want it," Izra stewed.

When we arrived home, I headed straight to our bar counter. I was furious at how close Keora was to us, but we couldn't react. I heard Goon's voice in the foyer, so I headed towards the basement door, but Anik pulled me back.

"You two cannot live like this. Talk to him. I will go and get the twins from Elle. I'm sure they kept him busy today," Anik said to me. I slowly walked into the foyer. My legs were getting wobbly. I was nervous when I approached him. Goon looked at me without any emotions. He didn't look happy or mad.

"Can we talk?" I asked him.

"Izra, grab me that muzzle out of the hall closet," Goon called out to him.

"Adika used it on me last night. Don't ask what we was doing. Just know that the muzzle ain't no good," Izra shouted back. Goon slightly chuckled.

“Follow me,” Goon said. We walked to the other end of the house that was nearly vacant. It looked like it wasn’t even a part of our home. We walked until we came upon a wooden door that was carved with hieroglyphs of men with wolf heads. There were other symbols I wasn’t familiar with. Goon grabbed my hand, and then we disappeared. We were on the other side of the door. The room was dark with candles lit. There were drawings carved into the floor and ancient masks that hung up on the walls.

I looked around, not knowing what room we were in and where it came from. “What is this?” I asked, touching the carvings on the wall.

“This is where I have been studying. The door doesn’t open. Only I can come in by disappearing to the other side of it,” Goon said to me as I looked around.

“You really are a warlock. This is so unbelievable,” I said to him as he towered over me.

“It’s not nowhere near as interesting as my beast,” he chuckled. Goon grabbed my hand then looked into my eyes. “Your beast is at peace with me now,” he said, caressing my cheek.

"I'm sorry I hurt you like that. I didn't want to do that. I even tried to shift back to human form, but it wouldn't allow me. She was so angry and uncontrollable. I was scared. If you want me to leave, I will," I said, not knowing what else to do.

"Your ass ain't going nowhere, but next time, stay away from my neck," he said to me chuckling. His smile warmed my heart. "If you want to kiss me, go on ahead. I won't bite unless you want me to," he said, pulling on my pants.

"Our relationship is going to always be dysfunctional, isn't it?"

"We are animals; we aren't normal. We cannot live like humans. That perfect relationship doesn't exist with our kind, but our bond and our love is stronger. Our minds are connected, and we are one, which makes our relationship stronger than any human relationship. I been forgave you. I was just wondering when you was going to stop hiding. You was peeking around corners and shit when you heard me coming." He laughed causing me to feel embarrassed.

"It's not funny. I was scared." Goon placed his hand on the back of my head and gripped my hair.

"You owe me some kisses." He bent down, attacking my lips. My hands went up to his broad shoulders. I slipped my tongue into his mouth, and his erection pressed down on my leg.

"I missed you," I said when I pulled away from him.

"I was right upstairs," he said, sliding my dress pants down."I like these," he said as he pulled on my lace thong. He turned me around then gently bit my left butt cheek. He gave it a firm smack, and his strong hands massaged my bottom while he placed kisses on each cheek. I held my breath when he slid my thong down, and his hand massaged my sex from the back. I was wet and I was throbbing. I wanted him to place himself inside of me.

You smell so good. My dick is about to burst out of my sweatpants, Goon said inside of my thoughts. I took off my blazer and my shirt as Goon unhooked my bra. I was naked with just my pumps on. My pussy clenched with thick nectar leaking from it. I squeezed my breasts. My nipples ached. Goon turned me around. He was still kneeling. He opened my slit, tasting my sweet essence, and he growled as he ate me. I held myself up by throwing my leg over his shoulders. He gripped me by the hips as he devoured my wet slit. I moaned then bit my lip. His tongue hungrily thrashed around my pussy. He then pulled my swollen bud into his mouth and groaned with pleasure. I wanted to please him; I wanted to taste him. He read my mind and stood up. I took his shirt off. I kissed his solid chest. Goon's body was perfectly sculpted, like someone took a sharp knife and carved his muscles into his body. My hands slid up his arms, arms that swallowed me when he hugged me. I kneeled down, pulling his sweatpants down along with his boxer briefs. His enormous dick sprang out, dripping with pre-cum. I stuck my tongue out then tasted him. I wrapped my mouth around him. He gripped my hair and slowly pumped into my mouth.

Your lips wrapped around my dick are about to make me burst, he said. I held him with both hands, sliding him in and out of my mouth, as spit ran down my chin. The strong veins in his shaft looked like they were ready to burst. His dick felt heavier as he grew harder.

"I need some pussy," he groaned, pulling me up. I got down on the floor, arching my back. Seconds later, Goon's big dick was penetrating me. He pressed down on my lower back, causing me to arch my back higher. He gripped my hips then slid in and out of me.

"Fuck me harder!" I screamed. His hands palmed each cheek, spreading me open, and he dived into my tight hole. My nails clawed the floor as he rammed himself in and out of me. The pressure shot up my spine and caused me to scream out. His nails dug into my hips as he hammered away, constantly hitting my spot over and over again. My nails shredded the rug with each thrust he gave me. My essence ran down my legs as Goon showed no mercy on me. He growled then groaned when my walls gripped him.

"OOOOOOOOOOHHHHHHHH," I moaned out loudly.

"GRRRRRRRRRRRRRR! FUCK!" Goon shouted out.

Sounds of him diving into my wet tunnel turned me on even more. Sweat ran down my back. My hair was stuck to my face. Goon gripped my wet hair, diving further into me, causing me to scream out loud. I had an orgasm that knocked the air out of me. I cried because the pleasure was too intense. The room spun when he put his weight on me, and I was laid flat on my stomach. He lifted himself up then wiggled his dick into me, my hole was tightening up on him.

"Open it up!" he growled, speeding up. I felt him jerk inside of me. I had an orgasm stronger than the first one. Goon bit my shoulder, enticing my orgasm. My body shook as he pumped his semen inside of me. He collapsed on top of me and nuzzled his nose into my neck. "I don't want to pull out of you. You're so warm and wet," his husky, deep voice said to me.

"I can't move!" I said, feeling squished. He stood up then helped me up.

"Let's go hunting. I just burned my whole meal off," he said getting dressed.

I yawned. "I'm too tired," I felt weak. I felt like I walked through a dry, hot desert for days without water.

"Your jackal always tests me, but when it comes to fucking, she is submissive," Goon laughed.

After I took a long shower, I bathed the twins then got them ready for bed. Goon came into the room with a tray of fresh raw meat with grapes and wine. I smiled because he always catered to me. He laid the tray down on our bed then fed me.

“Sometimes I feel like I don’t deserve you,” I said to him.

“Shut up and eat, Kanya. You are too dramatic at times. Just go with the flow.”

I realized all men are the same even if they have a beast in them; they don’t like emotional conversations. Goon walked out of my face a few times to avoid it.

“Tomorrow night, the pack is going to attack Dash’s pack. You will stay here along with Anik and Adika. It’s going to get ugly,” he said. I knew it was reason for him to be babying me up, he knew I was going to disagree with him.

“There are only five of you! You will get hurt.”

“They came on our territory and attacked us. We will attack them on theirs now. No life of theirs will be spared. It is going to get ugly, and the females stay here. As the

Alpha of this pack, it is my call, and no one will disobey my orders. It is already set in stone, and nothing you can do or say will change my mind."

"What if something happens to our brothers?"

"They are like warriors; they are bred to fight. They are fighters, and nothing will happen to them," he assured me then walked out of the room. I took out the stone that Anik gave me and squeezed onto it for dear life.

Keora

"Time is running out!" Saka yelled at me. I was tired of him. Goon's pack already knew what I was up to. They knew I was behind the attack on their territory. The gods may not know yet, but I was to the point where I no longer cared if they found out. Saka's dark cloud hovered over me inside of my sanctuary. He was angry with me, but I was even angrier at myself. I no longer had the desire to be Saka's puppet.

"Would you shut the fuck up? It was me who brought you back, and I can send you back to the dark world I took you out of!"

"I will see you in hell when the gods send you there," he said, disappearing. When Saka left, I felt a pain surge through my stomach that caused me to scream out. I looked to the corner, and his spell books were gone; he took the black magic away from me. I was no longer shielded. The gods could see and hear my thoughts.

I grabbed a few of my things, packing them into a sack. I also grabbed a few potions and a few of my old spell books. I was going to hide until I figured out my next plan.

"Where are you going?" a voice said from behind me. I dropped my things then turned around. Naobi stared at me with glowing, green eyes. I backed away into the corner. "My dear, dear child," she said to me, floating closer. "I gave you life and this is what you do? You betrayed Anubi; you betrayed me. I loved you like a daughter. I taught you spells, and you used them against me?"

"You took Akua away from me when you knew I loved him," I said to her.

"Bow down on your hands and feet when you speak with me," she said staring down at me. I kneeled down on the floor. "I created you and Adika ages ago to protect and shield Akua from Saka. I didn't create you to bed my child," she said raising her voice. The glass in my house shattered, and my house shook, knocking items onto the floor.

"You love Dayo, but Dayo doesn't love you. He was cursed; you tricked him. The feelings he has for you will no longer exist!" The floor in my house cracked, and a shining gold light emerged from the cracks. "I will see you in Anubi where you will become a prisoner for eternity," Naobi said to me, and then she and I disappeared.

*****

I sat in a prison like the one I made for Dayo. One of the servants sat bread and water by the bars. Naobi came by the bars smirking at me, holding up a small globe.

"You have been very busy," she said as she watched Dayo give me pleasure inside of the club bathroom inside of the globe. It was like a television to her of all my wrong doings.

"Oh, this one is my favorite. Very clever girl. You wanted to find out about Kanya so you disguised yourself as an old woman." She watched the globe as I disguised myself as a patient at the nursing home Kanya worked at.

Then she showed me another one of me putting something inside of Kanya's chocolate milk before she mated. I was going to poison Kanya, but she poured the milk out.

She put the globe in her sack then pulled out a thin stone sheet with old Egyptian drawings on it.

"Some of the wolves' ancestors created this; they saw visions of the future life. They engraved their visions on the walls of their temples and even these sheets of rock. Akua's future was seen and so was Dayo's. You see, Dayo has a soul mate, and it is not you. He doesn't realize it yet, but Anik found him. A force brought her into his territory. All that is happening between Dayo and Anik was predicted ages and ages ago. Anik's tribe helped Egyptians, for Indians had medicine that could cure an injured warrior, making us all like family ages ago. Dayo's ancestor had a vision and drew it, and just like the prediction, Anik found him. You cannot interfere with the god's visions," Naobi said to me as tears fell down my face.

Then she saw the vision of me pretending to be a male costumer that showed interest in Anik. I told her I was looking for a necklace for my grandmother. I was going to get her away from the pack and cast her away.

"What do the humans say on earth? Oh yeah, that was really cute, bitch," Naobi said to me then chuckled.

"Well, I have to go and catch up with what you have been doing," Naobi said, walking away.

"I bet you haven't told Kaira that her pup doesn't belong to Kofi. He belongs to Ammon. I guess it was your magic that made Dash look like Kofi, disguising him as someone else's pup. That's the real reason why you don't want Kiara to see him; a mother can sense who her pup belongs to. I bet that's why you refuse to show your mate any affection. I guess Kofi's mate being raped and Kaira being in heat was the perfect alibi. It was you who made them fuck to cover up your piece of shit mate!" I said to Naobi.

"Don't you see? This was never about Akea. Although Saka wanted him, I wanted you to feel what I have been feeling since you took Akua away from me. I want Ammon to resent you, and he will because Akua is going to kill his own brother. And whose fault is it going to be? Perhaps yours because Ammon doesn't even know he has a son. If

Dash dies, you will be in an immortal prison," I said to Naobi then smirked.

"Unlike you, I can get out. Clever witch, might I add. I trained you well. But I want to show you something," Naobi said.

She held up her globe, and there I saw a vision of me talking to Saka. He disappeared, and then I bent over because a pain surged through my stomach.

"A witch's pup with wolf blood. Seems like Saka got what he wanted. How does it feel to carry a demon pup inside of your womb? Days of torture await you. Saka didn't give a damn about Akea after you bedded Dayo; he knew you was pregnant. Why do you think Saka left so easily? He tricked you, Keora, and after all of this, you are the one who is left without a mate. Never negotiate with an evil witch; they always have more than one plan," Naobi said then disappeared.

Naobi

I sat in my sanctuary watching visions of Akua and his pack preparing to attack Dash's pack. Dash was an Alpha, but he wasn't made like Akua. My blood that runs through Akua's veins is what makes him stronger. I have been so focused on Akua that I let everything else slip pass me. I walked out of my sanctuary then down the hall to where Ammon was talking to a warrior. Ammon looked at me and smiled.

"Good evening, beautiful," Ammon said to me. I excused the warrior he was speaking with then grabbed Ammon's hand. I led him to a doorway that overlooked the sparkling lake that surrounded our temple."What concerns you?" Ammon asked me.

"Keora knows something about me that I haven't shared with you," I said to him.

"What is that? Is Akua okay?"

"He is fine. You know what I have realized? Having power and strength doesn't take away our flaws nor does it make our life as immortals perfect. Sometimes I look at my globe and watch humans; they live freely. They make many mistakes, but they live without rules. In Anubi, we live by rules, and I just want to be free."

"What are you speaking about, Naobi?"

"I remember the day you were bitten by a wolf. That was the day you found out I was a witch. You were a human and lived freely. I use to watch you throw your spears under the sunlight with the other warriors. I knew when I first saw you that I loved you. When you were human, you made me feel like I was human. The day you got bitten, I tried to save you with a spell, but I cursed you for eternity instead. But I loved you so much that I couldn't watch you die. I gave you life again, and you mated with Kaira behind my back! She had a pup, and it belonged to you; his name is Dash. Akua and his pack are ready to attack him; they are going to kill him. A part of me wants Akua to rip him apart since he came from another wolf. But I couldn't live with that. You need to go to earth to stop your pups from fighting," I said to Ammon. Tears welled up in his eyes, and then I walked away. "The gates are open and waiting for you," I said to him then disappeared.

I will be with you soon, I said into his head, but he didn't respond. He was tired of waiting, and I no longer wanted him to.

Goon

I howled when I got onto Dash's land. My pack stood behind me with their tribal markings etched through their fur. Dash and his pack emerged from the trees; there were about nine of them. Dash growled at me with his ears pointed back.

You come onto my territory? My pups got hurt because of your pack. You was helping Keora to take my pup. Your pack will all die tonight! I said to Dash.

We do many things but taking pups isn't one of them. Keora never stated what she wanted; she just needed the distraction. I had to do what I had to do to support my pack.

Although he said he didn't know Keora wanted Akea, I still howled. My pack charged into his pack, ripping them apart. Dash and I circled around each other. I used my spells to make my pack stronger and heal faster. More wolves came, even his mate. Amilia attacked Elle, and

Amadi ripped her throat out. Dash tried to charge Amadi, but I charged at him first. We clawed and bit each other. I slung him by the neck into a tree. The tree fell onto one of his wolves, breaking its neck. Dash got up then charged into me, and I sank my teeth into his face. Jalesa appeared out of nowhere. She jumped onto Amadi's back with a gold-like sphere that turned some of the wolves into ashes. A wolf jumped on my back with his teeth in my neck. Then three more leaped on me as we rolled around on the ground. They savagely tried to pull me apart. My teeth sharpened. Gold appeared around my neck, legs and arms. I was in my ancient form. I slashed one wolf's neck then the others stomach. More tried to take me down, but I was stronger. Dash got a hold of my neck, but I shook him off then charged into him. My teeth pierced through his neck, and blood squirted into my mouth and dripped from my fur. I was going to kill him, but a force knocked me into a tree. The wolves stopped fighting. My father's larger wolf stood in the middle.

My father was all black with blue eyes. He had gold Egyptian beads hanging from his mane and a gold and blue shield around his shoulders. Dash tried to get up, but I charged into him, trying to kill him. My father's huge beast charged into me, knocking me off Dash. When I got back up, he stood in front of Dash as he lay on the ground bleeding from his neck.

I will fight you, Father, if I have to in order to finish him off, I said into his thoughts. My pack stood behind me growling. They were willing to disobey the gods in order to protect me.

He is your brother, and I cannot let you kill him.

That isn't my concern. My concern is for my pups. You are protecting your pup just like I'm doing mines. His pack attacked mines even on my territory. His wolves ambushed my mate while our pups were in the vehicle. Brother or not, I have no sympathy for him. I'm going to kill him.

That isn't going to happen! he said, and then he and Dash disappeared. I howled as loud as I could with my pack howling behind me. I was pissed off.

When we got home, I shifted back to human form then hurriedly put my sweatpants on. The females came into the den checking on us.

"I was worried. Thank heavens everyone is safe," Kanya said, placing kisses all over my face.

"What happened?" Adika asked.

"Goon's daddy been fucking other bitches," Izra said.

"Bro, not now," Elle said to Izra.

"I'm not going to sit here and pretend that big, black muthafucka didn't just come out of nowhere to defend Dash. I want to know how that nigga is Goon's brother. I thought Naobi only had one son. I didn't know wolves could mate on the outside," Izra said.

"Don't get any ideas from it neither. You want to know a little bit too much," Adika scolded Izra.

"Shut the hell up, Adika. I been faithful. You keep bringing up old shit," Izra spat and I shook my head.

"Shut the hell up and let us think. You talk too damn much," Dayo said to him.

"Nigga, you shut up! It's all your fault anyway. You shouldn't had been fucking that old mummy! Her ass wasn't even phat," Izra shouted at Dayo. Dayo socked Izra in the eye, and then Izra slammed into Dayo. They started throwing punches at each other. Anik, Adika, Amadi and Elle tried to pull them apart as they pummeled each other.

I walked into the kitchen, grabbed a bottle of Henny, then gulped it down like water. Kanya came in behind me and started to massage my shoulders.

"I'm sure the answers you are looking for will come out soon," Kanya said to me.

"Honestly, I don't care for any. Whatever they have going on in Anubi is their business. My pack and my pups on this earth are my only concern. I could have dozens of siblings, and it will not matter to me."

"There has to be a way around this. You don't want to kill your brother if he really is your brother," Kanya said. I pulled away from her after there was a loud knock on my door.

"Who in the hell got over the gate and didn't get ashed?" Adika asked.

"It must be one of the gods," Jalesa said then disappeared.

“That witch is very weird, bro,” Dayo said to Amadi.

I rushed to the door then opened it. My father was dressed in a long, gold silk shirt with matching pants. The medallion around his neck shined.

“Can I come in?” he asked in his heavy accent.

“Damn, he iced out,” Izra said. Adika slapped his arm.

“That is Ammon. Show some respect,” Adika scolded Izra.

I opened up the door wider to let him in. Ammon walked in looking around. “I saw visions of your temple, but this is very interesting,” he said. Everyone bowed their heads when my father walked in.

“Can I get you anything?” Kanya asked my father.

“Your mate is a servant?” my father asked me.

“No, she isn’t. This is our way of living,” I answered bluntly.

“You have your pack brothers around your mate? That is forbidden in Anubi,” my father said to me.

“So is fucking other wolves,” I heard Dayo mumble underneath his breath. Elle growled at Dayo, but he just shrugged his shoulders. I wondered what Ammon would've done if he knew what Dayo was saying.

My father followed me down the hall into the library. I closed the doors then told him to take a seat.

"You need to obey orders, son," he said to me when I sat down across from him.

"I don't obey anything when there is a cause behind my actions. Dash was behind what Keora was doing, and anyone who is behind her is against me."

"Fair enough."

"How did you mate outside of my mother?"

"Kaira was in heat, and it was hard to resist her. The same way it was hard for Xavier to resist Kanya. Wolves can mate on the outside, but they can only have one mate. Naobi is who I will spend all my life with, but a strong scent will catch the nose of any wolf. I'm different than you. You were born a wolf. I was born human then was turned into a wolf. Then Naobi and I fell in love. She and I weren't soul mates. Our ancestors didn't have visions of us together. I was a human man who was supposed to live a human life."

"Why do Kofi and Dash look alike?"

"Your mother disguised him so I wouldn't know I had a pup. She didn't want Kaira to know Dash belonged to me. Kofi was with Kaira also," he said shamefully.

"Anubi is just like earth then."

"Only difference between humans and immortals is that we don't age."

"So, Dash's mother is a hoe?" I asked him.

"A hoe?"

"A woman who beds many men."

"She is a jezebel," he said.

"How do you know he belongs to you?" I asked him.

"You can sense your pups when you are around them. I know he is my son."

"He isn't my brother. My brothers are in my pack. I will kill him if I see him again. He will be joining his mate pretty soon. I will show no mercy on him after he heals. I will be ready to take him out, and nobody is going to stop me."

"I will not allow that to happen. You will obey my orders. You and he will have to make peace."

I chuckled. “We will just have to wait and see.”

“Dash will remain in Anubi. We are against killing those who have the same blood as us,” he said, standing up.

“Where is my other brother? Dash has a twin, right?”

“Only mated soul mates have twin pups. Mated soul mates don’t mate on the outside. They are spiritually bonded; they are connected. Your mate’s scent will always overpower another female wolf, even if the female wolf is in heat,” he said.

“Uncle Goon, can I feed the pups? It’s my turn, remember?” Arya barged into the room. I picked her up then tickled her stomach.

“Arya, this is my father, Ammon. Ammon, this is Arya. She is the youngest pack member.”

Ammon gave Arya a handful of rubies. “When you get older, you have your mate bring you the finest gems,” he told Arya.

“Then I can have pups?” she asked Ammon.

“Anik! Get your ass in here,” I called out to her. Anik came into the room.

"What happened?" she asked nervously while staring at my father. He did appear to be a bit intimidating.

"I thought I told you to have that pup talk with her."

"How can I when I don't know anything about that myself?" Anik asked me. She grabbed Arya's hand then stormed out of the library.

"Chippewa wolves are good company, very spiritual. Before my time runs out visiting, I would like to see the pups," he said to me.

He followed me to the family room where Kanya and Adika were feeding the pups. Kanya and Adika gave the pups to my father, and he held them.

"I haven't held a pup in ages," he said. He stayed a while then left. He promised to visit again when he could.

*****

I lay across the bed on my stomach. Kanya sat on my back massaging it. I growled, falling asleep. "Amadi's oil is relaxing, isn't it?" she asked, squirting more on my back.

The fire from the fireplace warmed the room, and the house was quiet. Kanya's small hands gripped every muscle in my back.

"GOON! Don't go to sleep," she shouted, waking me up.

"I'm tired."

"We are supposed to be having a romantic night tonight." She leaned over then nibbled on my ear. "What do you think is going to happen to Saka?"

"I don't know. I let the gods deal with everything else. All this shit is their problem anyway. As long as no harm comes to this pack, I'm not worried. They need to keep all that shit up there," I said and Kanya giggled.

"My Goonie," she said, biting my ear. I bit my bottom lip then turned over. I pulled Kanya on top of me and nuzzled my nose into her neck. I palmed her round ass cheeks.

"UMPH," I said, pressing my hard dick into her leg. Her kinky tendrils fell into her face, and I moved them away. "Will you marry me?" I asked her.

"You already asked me," she said, licking my lips.

"No, I didn't. I told you I was going to marry you then gave you the ring. We had an argument, and I wasn't going to ask you that shit."

"I have been rocking this rock on my finger, and we wasn't engaged?"

"It looks good on your finger, beautiful. That's all that mattered," I said to her. I opened up her robe, and her big, round breasts popped out. She lifted her bottom up then grabbed my dick. She slowly slid down onto my length. Her eyes turned gold, and her fangs sharpened. Tiny gold hairs pierced through her skin; her hair was wild and bushy. Her nails dug into my chest as she slowly rode me, and I gripped her hips. Her pussy was flooding. Her walls choked my dick, causing me to growl out loud. I massaged her breasts, thrusting upwards into her. Her eyes rolled into her head.

Are you about to cum already?" I said in her mind.

I feel you in my stomach, she replied back. I pulled her forward then kissed her lips. I held onto her as I thrust into her dripping wet sex. Her breasts bounced in my face. I captured her nipple biting into it. She growled then moaned as her body shook. I wasn't too far behind. Moments later, I came inside of her. Kanya fell onto my chest, and I pulled the blanket over us. I wrapped my arms around her, swallowing her in my embrace. Her hair was sprawled out all over my chest.

"I love you, Goon," she said to me.

"I love you too," I said, closing my eyes.

Naobi

I walked into the room where Dash rested. Ammon had healed him and brought Dash and Dash's pups to Anubi because Goon's pack had killed his mate.

"I see you aren't as tough as your father," I said to him. He slowly sat up. He no longer looked like Kofi. He resembled Akua and Ammon. The spell was off. There wasn't any use for it, although I would rather him look like anyone else but Ammon and Akua.

"You disguised me," Dash said to me.

"It could've been worse," I told him. I walked around him. He was naked with only a sheet wrapped around his waist. I wanted to examine what Ammon had created behind my back. Dash had the same body structure, but he was a little shorter than Akua. Akua was built more like a warrior, maybe because Akua was older.

"Goon's pack killed my mate," Dash said with anger.

"A real Alpha would not allow his mate to fight in a battle with male wolves. You killed your mate."

"You poisoned Xavier. I saw you come to the house. You were a bartender at his club."

"A mother knows best. Why are you here?"

"Ammon brought me here," he spat.

"He will be living here," Ammon's voice boomed from behind me.

"What?" I asked Ammon.

"His pack is dead and so is his mate. There is no place on earth for him," Ammon said to me.

My eyes watered, and then I screamed. Ammon fell onto the floor and so did Dash. Blood ran from their noses and ears while they yelled out in pain.

"STOP IT!" Ammon yelled. Things in the room started flying against the wall. Kaira ran into the room.

"What is that noise?" she asked. Her body went soaring into the stone wall. Then she came crashing onto the floor with blood running from her head. I stopped screaming and watched Ammon. He looked worried about her, and I saw his vision of him helping her up.

"If you touch her, I will kill her, and then I will kill you," I said to him. His eyes turned blue as he growled.

"What is happening to you?" Ammon asked me.

"When the moon settles over the river, I will be gone for eternity. Kofi and Opal ran into the room.

"What is going on?" Kofi asked, helping Kaira up. Dash crawled onto the bed then lay down, breathing heavily.

"You are evil!" Kaira said to me, holding her head.

I walked out of the room then down the long temple hall.

"Naobi, come quick! Something is wrong with your prisoner," A warrior said to me. I followed him down the long spiral staircase. He gave me his torch for lighting. Keora lay on the prison floor sweating with her stomach moving.

"Help me," she said weakly.

"Help you with what?" I asked her.

"My baby, you need to save my baby."

"That is not a baby! That is Saka! He trapped himself inside of your womb. Your baby is dead! We witches cannot carry live babies in our wombs. Our power sucks the life out of babies. They are too weak to withstand all that we do. It doesn't allow them to grow, and it eventually kills them," I said to her then she screamed.

"Go get the Musaf. Tell him we have a demon that is trapped," I said to the warrior. He bowed his head then ran up the staircase with his sphere in his hand.

"What are you going to do to me?" Keora asked weakly.

"Something I should've been done centuries ago."

Musaf came down the stairs dressed in a lion's skin. The lion's head hung over his aged face, covering his eyes. Musaf's skin was the color of black oil, and he had a crocodile tooth pierced through his bottom lip. Musaf has been around for thousands of years, longer than I've existed. He was an old warlock. Although witches couldn't carry babies, warlocks could give them. Musaf had thousands of daughters. He appeared on the inside of the cage. He lifted up Keora's shirt. He put a red, lumpy paste onto her stomach then her forehead. He rattled his weird instrument that had dead animal skins hanging from it and then said something in a different language.

"ARRGGGGHHHHHHHHHHHHHH!" Keora screamed. Musaf pulled her pants down, opened her legs and began to chant.

"It hurts!" Keora screamed as Musaf chanted. Keora cried as her baby came from between her legs. The baby was alive. Pups only stayed in the womb for two months. Musaf caused Keora to have it early, so the baby was small.

"Give me my baby!" Keora said, trying to sit up, but as she reached for it, Musaf disappeared. "What did you do?" she cried.

"That baby is not your baby. Once Saka's soul comes out of it, the baby will die. The baby wasn't meant to live," I said to her.

"I'm sorry! I'm sorry!" Keora cried.

"I know you are, but it's time to send Saka to a world where he will be trapped." As I walked out of the dungeon, Keora cried and screamed. I walked outside of the temple into a small stone house. Musaf held the baby in his arms sprinkling some dust over it. A dark cloud hovered over us.

"You have been very busy, Father," I said. Keora's pup closed its eyes; Saka's soul could no longer keep it alive."What is it that you want?" I asked him.

"I want my body!" his voice shouted.

"I cannot give you that. I kept you in spirit because you are my father, but even in spirit you are still dangerous. It's time I let you go."

"I am your father!" he screamed.

"Good-bye, Father." Musaf pulled out a gold urn, and it sucked the small black cloud up. Musaf was going to send my father to hell where he belonged. I patted Musaf's shoulders, and he nodded his head at me. Musaf didn't talk much. He mostly stayed in his sanctuary practicing voodoo.

"Where have you been? You cannot roam the temple all night by yourself," Ammon said to me when I returned back to the temple.

"I have been taking care of unfinished business," I said to him. Ammon caressed my face.

"I miss you, Naobi." He pulled me into him, and a tear slipped from my eye.

"I'm leaving this temple," I said to him.

"Not without my permission. You will remain here. You are my mate, and you will act like one!" Ammon shouted at me with his eyes turning.

I touched his face. "My dear Ammon. My wolf god. It's time for me to depart from this temple and live amongst the free. I will live in my sanctuary far away from here. You will always have desire for a wolf who can birth your pups. I did my job; I kept you alive, and I gave you a powerful son. Akua will be the next ruler in Anubi hundreds and hundreds of years from now. He will be a powerful one."

"You have desires like a human. You will serve as my mate, Naobi. What do you want? You want what the humans on earth have? Since you have been watching Akua on earth you've changed! What have you become, huh? You are a witch. You will never have and feel what humans feel," Ammon fussed.

"They hold hands, make love, kiss on the lips, sleep holding each other. They have romance; they have each other. It's a beautiful feeling. Immortals can live that way, but everything we do is because of rules. Women walk around their mates naked and free. I would be called a jezebel if I walked around you like that. When you enter me, I cannot touch you. I have to lay still and let you have your way with me. You have an outside pup, and his pups are living in our temple along with his mother. You have a family here that I will not be a part of. You have forgotten where you came from. You came from humans. How dare you look down on them," I said to him.

"You will be banished if you use that tone with me."

"What is that word Kanya uses on Akua when she is upset? Oh yeah, that's right. Fuck you."

Ammon's nostrils flared. He charged into me, but a force pulled him back. He had a chain around his neck that was connected to the wall. Ammon was in wolf form, and he howled while trying to pull away from the chain that was around his neck.

"You will be released when the sun peaks over the river," I said, walking out. I put the hood on my cape over my head. I grabbed my spells books then put them into my sack. I went down into the dungeon to release Keora, but she wasn't free.

"Where are you taking me?" Keora asked me.

"You think I would leave you here? You are stuck with me until you become pure again. Evil still lurks around the hatred in your heart. When you become pure, I will erase everything from your mind. You will live how I see fit, but not as a witch. Now come. I have work to do."

"My hands are locked together," Keora complained.

"And they will remain that way," I said, pulling her up the stairs. Kofi and Opal walked towards us.

"Promise us that you will stay in our visions," Kofi said to me. I grabbed his hand.

"Of course. I will miss the both of you, and if you need me, I will know." I then hugged Opal. After I said my goodbyes Keora and I disappeared.

*****

"What basement are we in?" Keora asked in her prison.

"It doesn't matter," I said to her as I sat in my chair watching my small globe. I smiled as I watched Akua and Kanya play around in the woods. Their beasts rolled around on the ground with each other. Kanya licked his ear, and he rubbed his head under her neck.

"This is what you call love, Keora. You shouldn't have to cast spells to get it."

"Why are you this way?" Keora asked me.

"My mother was a human. Warlocks impregnate human women. The female witches are born infertile, but the male witches aren't. My mother got old and died. I watched her from afar when I was a little girl. Saka took me from her when I was a baby to raise me to be powerful. I watched her for years as her age progressed. She lived to be ninety years old. I visited her on her death bed, but she didn't know who I was. I told her I was her daughter. She said my daughter should be gray. I looked to be only fifteen years old. So, I made a way for the Egyptians to live for eternity. I should've reincarnated her after she died, but I didn't know how to use spells back then," I said to Keora, and a tear slipped from Keora's eye.

I looked around my new home. I was far away from Ammon's palace. I didn't have warriors roaming around for protection. It was just Keora and I. I snapped my fingers, and a meal of chicken, fruit and wine appeared. Keora looked at the food.

"Are you trying to poison me?" Keora asked me, which made me chuckle.

"If I do that, then Adika will die. Your punishment is fair enough. I never thought my own creation would turn out this way. I created you and her with love from my heart."

"What the hell is that?" Keora asked, pointing behind me. An oversized tiger walked into my sanctuary. His eyes glowed green.

I smiled. "That is Kumba," I said, rubbing the tiger's head. A gold medallion was embedded into his chest, and gold bangles were wrapped around his legs. Keora backed away in her prison; she was scared.

Kumba shifted into human form, and there he stood—tall, dark and strong. He was about six foot eight in height, and his chest and shoulders were broad. His skin was the color of honey, and his face was strong and strikingly handsome. His green eyes looked down at me.

"My beautiful, Naobi. I'm glad to see you home. I have been waiting a long time for you," Kumba said to me.

"Who the hell is that and what's going on? Are you going to feed me to him?" Keora asked. I pulled out a thin sheet of stone with drawings on it. I walked towards her cage-like prison then dropped the sheet inside. Keora picked it up and read the drawings. "Your human mother's ancestors had a vision of you with a tiger warrior? Ammon isn't going to stand back. He will sense when someone else enters you. Send me back to earth. I don't want any parts of this shit."

Kumba laughed. "She is something else."

"Why does he speak fine English?" Keora asked me.

“We are on earth,” I said to her.

“You are weak on earth,” Keora said to me, and then I laughed.

“That’s what I wanted Ammon to think. If he knew all I was capable of, I would be considered a threat to Anubi.”

“Ammon isn’t going to allow this. You and I both know it!”

“We will wait and see,” I said to her. I walked out of the basement then upstairs. Kumba followed behind me wearing only black silk pants. He had black, thick markings across his chest resembling his tiger. I have been connecting with Kumba in my secret sanctuary back in Anubi. He had visions of me in his dreams where I appeared. He touched my face.

“You are even more beautiful in person. You look very young,” he chuckled. Kumba wasn’t an ancestor of my creation. He was an ancestor of one of Musaf’s offspring who was into voodoo using cats.

I touched him. He looked to be in his mid-thirties in human years.

"Show me around," I said to him. He grabbed my hand then walked me around his home. It was smaller than Ammon's temple, but it felt like home. It felt warm; it felt like life lived in it. There weren't any rules, just he and I. Kumba owned a chain of restaurants that cooked African foods. He doesn't age, so he barely shows his face. When he had to, I disguised him.

He opened up a door. "This is our bedroom. It's different than what you are used to, but you will adjust." I looked around. I walked into another room that was connected to his.

"What is that?" I asked him. He came in then turned a knob. Water came out into a big, white-shaped octagon.

"That is a Jacuzzi. I sit in it to relax."

"Do I take my clothes off?" I asked him.

"If you want to," he chuckled. I got undressed then stood in front of him naked. He didn't look at me like I had committed a sin. He looked at me with lust. His strong hands covered my breasts. Goosebumps formed on my arms. My body temperature rose, and I started to panic.

"What is happening?" I asked him.

"You are aroused," he said to me. Kumba was very tall, like a giant. He picked me up so I could be eye level with him. His lips came to mine, and he slipped his tongue inside of my mouth. My legs wrapped around him. He pulled his pants down, dropping them to his ankles. He climbed inside of the tub with me, and the water bubbled.

I was straddling him as his length grew underneath me. I throbbed uncontrollably like I never had throbbed before. I needed him inside of me. He lifted me up then slowly slid himself inside of me. Kumba took my breast inside of his mouth. I didn't know if what he was doing was wrong, but it was a feeling I had never had before. My body trembled. I didn't know what to do.

"You feel so beautiful," Kumba whispered in my ear as he thrust upwards inside of me. A moan slipped from my lips, followed by many others. Kumba's size stretched me open. With every thrust, I felt connected to him. A tear slid out of my eye. I missed thousands and thousands of years of this feeling. His tongue flickered across my swollen nipple. I cried out. His nails extended, cutting into my skin. The water splashed out of the tub, and Kumba purred. My secret place gripped his girth, causing my body to tremble as I screamed out. The glass in his mirrors cracked, and the light in the room blew out. Kumba throbbed. Then I felt something shoot up inside of me. He kissed my lips then smirked, showing a set of white teeth with very long canines. "I would've lasted longer, but you gripped the hell out of me," he said, kissing my neck.

"It's supposed to last longer?"

"On earth, we call it stamina."

"What does that mean?"

"Making love for a long period of time without getting tired." He then gave me a serious look. "Will your pup approve of me? I have met a few werewolves, and they aren't the easiest to get along with."

"Akua is very grumpy, but I have a feeling his mate will scold him. She is very feisty, and he lets her get her way," I said laughing.

"What about Ammon? Do you still love him?"

"I love him because he gave me my son, who I love more than life, but Ammon and I aren't destined to be. I gave him many years, and yet I still felt incomplete."

“Let me out of here!” Keora screamed and we chuckled.

“You are an evil witch,” Kumba said, kissing my nose.

“With a lot of love to give.”

Kanya

The holidays were approaching, and Beastly Treasures was crowded. Goon walked around interacting with costumers. He wore his tailored suit, and it fit his body perfectly. I stared at him like I had never seen him before. The way he walked, his stride and his appearance screamed alpha. He was my alpha, my beast.

Goon walked over to me then bent down to whisper in my ear. “How dare you get an arousal around all of these people. Now I want to taste you,” he said, causing me to blush.

“Cut it out. I’m glad you’ve been talking to me normally and not popping up in my head. You know that shit still scares me sometimes, right?” I asked him, and then he chuckled.

A man and a woman walked into the store. The man was very tall, like a basketball player. The woman seemed familiar; I remembered that walk. Her walk was smooth and seductive, like her feet didn't touch the floor. The couple walked over to Goon and me. The tall guy had a scent of an animal—an animal I wasn't familiar with. A growl slipped out of our throats. When the couple got closer to us, I realized it was Naobi. She looked normal. She wasn't in her thick, ancient jewelry or her fancy silk garments. She was dressed in a pair of jeans, a sweater and riding boots. Her hair was braided up in some type of updo, and her face was so youthful.

When Naobi got closer to Goon, she reached out then hugged him. She planted kisses all over his cheeks. A smirk spread across Goon's face until he looked at the tall man his mother was with.

"That isn't my father," Goon said to Naobi.

"This is Kumba. Kumba, this is my son, Akua."

"We can go to my office and talk," I said, and they followed me into the back. Goon looked like he wanted to shift; he kept growling. When we got to my office, I hurriedly closed the door.

“Who are you and what are you to my mother?” Goon asked.

Kumba chuckled. “I’m your mother’s mate.”

“You aren’t a werewolf. What are you?” Goon asked him.

“I’m a tiger,” Kumba said.

“So, this is why my father said he mated on the outside. You had no connectional bond with him because you had a mate?” Goon asked his mother.

“Yes,” Naobi said sadly. Goon looked Kumba up and down. “He speaks without an Anubi accent. Does he live amongst the humans too?” Goon asked her.

“Yes, he does, and so do I. I left Anubi.”

“You can do that?” I asked her.

“I can do a lot. If we stay on earth for a long time, we are locked out of Anubi, but I have no reason to go back. Where is Jalesa? I need to tell her that she doesn’t have to go back.”

“She and Amadi were last seen bringing some oil in,” I said to Naobi. Izra and Dayo barged into my office.

"There is an animal in here," Dayo said with Izra growling.

"It's me," Kumba said, not feeling the least bit of a threat.

"You like cats anyway, don't you?" Goon asked Izra.

"Very funny, nigga. This big muthafucka isn't a cat," Izra stated rudely.

"He is a tiger, and watch your tongue," Naobi scolded Izra.

"Oh, what's up, Naobi? I didn't know that was you. You look normal. I'm surprised you aren't dressed like those people in that movie *Coming to America*," Izra said.

Dayo pushed Izra into the wall. "This is one ignant jackass," Dayo said about Izra.

Kumba laughed. "Quite a pack you got here."

Goon eased up. "Keep her happy so I won't get any more markings. Every time she cries, I get one, and it hurts like hell," Goon joked.

"Where is Keora?" I asked Naobi.

"In her dungeon. You will not see her anymore or hear from Saka," she assured me. Naobi gave us her address, and she promised to see us soon. Then she and Kumba left.

"She seemed so normal even though her presence is still strong," I said to Goon.

"I noticed that," Goon said. I fixed his tie.

"I'm proud of you. You didn't leap on Kumba even though you wanted to," I said to him.

"I didn't feel like hearing your yacking in my head. You women are very sensitive when it comes to love. Besides, I'm looking forward to this honeymoon you spoke of after we get married. A week away from the pack; it will just be you and I having more pups."

"I'm not in heat."

"Well, I'm going to pretend that you are and fuck the living shit out of you," he said in his husky voice.

"I need to separate you from Dayo and Izra," I said, walking out of the office. Goon reached out then grabbed my bottom, and I swatted his hand away.

Anastasia switched over to me, slinging his short, edgy cut. "Kanya, darrliinnggggggg, I have been looking all over for you," he sang out. He pulled me to the side.

"We are very busy," I said to him.

"I know, but I was wondering if you want a three-layer cake or a four-layer cake for the wedding?" Anastasia asked me. He was a god send. He helped me with my store and was helping me plan a wedding. Adika said she could give me the wedding of the century with her spells, but I wanted to experience it like a normal woman. I wanted to do things the traditional way.

"It doesn't matter. Nobody in my house eats cake, but make sure we have a lot of red meat, slightly cooked. I mean, a lot of rare meat," I said to Anastasia.

"You sure you aren't a wolf? I swear you guys remind me of werewolves. I'm infatuated with them. Don't you just hate that we have to live like humans? I want to jump in a *Twilight* book and screw Jacob's brains out," Anastasia said. Then I laughed.

"You have quite an imagination," I said to him.

"I know. That's why I'm gay. Nothing is normal in my world," he joked, swinging his hair and making me laugh.

My cell phone rang, and it was my mother. I excused myself from Anastasia to answer my phone.

"Hello," I sang sweetly into the phone.

"I'm sorry, Kanya. Your father still refuses to come to your wedding."

"But why?" I asked her.

"He doesn't want you to marry Akua. He said that Akua is a thug and is going down the road of destruction. I tried to talk him into it, but he still refuses. I'm sorry, honey."

"Thank you, Mom. I love you, and I appreciate you and everything you do." After I hung up with my mother, I walked back inside of my office and cried. It felt like my father had turned his back on me. He was supposed to give me away.

"What's the matter?" Anik's voice asked me. "I saw you rush off." She sat down in front of me.

"My father doesn't want anything to do with me," I said to her.

"Oh, screw him. You have your mother and the pack. Goon isn't going anywhere, so your father will just have to deal with it."

"I guess you are right." I looked in the mirror to make sure my mascara wasn't running. Anik started sweating profusely. "What's the matter with you?" I asked her.

"I'm uncomfortable. I'm having spasms down below," she said, fanning herself.

"You are in heat. You need to have sex, and if you don't, it will only get worse."

"I'm saving myself for my mate."

"Maybe Dayo is your mate. You took to him quickly, soon as you met him. You ended up on our territory for a reason. I believe it was fate."

"He doesn't pay attention to me," Anik said sadly.

"He was cursed, but I think he does pay attention to you. He doesn't even allow any of the male costumers to talk to you." I laughed and she blushed.

"What does it feel like? Does it hurt?" Anik asked me. I wanted to lie to her and tell her it didn't so it wouldn't scare her, but I couldn't.

"Yes, but after a while it goes away, but with Goon, it still hurts like it's my first time. I had been with another man before I met Goon," I said.

*****

Later on that night, Goon and I lay in our bed tangled up in each other. His hand rubbed my back as he kissed me. We couldn't keep our hands off each other. There was a big bang in our house. It sounded like someone broke into our home. Goon jumped out of bed then shifted. I shifted right after then ran after him down the stairs. In our foyer was a big black wolf with menacing blue eyes. He was bigger than Goon's beast. The big black wolf had gold bangles around its legs and beads in its mane. He had three wolves behind him. I knew it was Ammon.

Where is my mate? Ammon asked inside of our thoughts. The rest of the pack ran down the stairs in wolf form, growling. Adika shifted into her Egyptian Mau. She stood next to me purring with her ears going back while her back was humped.

She isn't here. How dare you barge into our home, breaking our door down, while my pups are asleep. This isn't Anubi. You will show respect for our territory, Goon said.

My warriors will search your temple. I will not leave until she reveals herself. The gates to Anubi will close soon, and I will do what I have to do to get her."

Adika paced back and forth growling because one of Ammon's warriors was growling at her. The warrior snapped at Adika. She charged into him, clawing his face. The wolf bit Adika, and Izra charged into him, knocking him into the wall.

Goon's eyes glowed and so did the tribal markings in his fur. Ammon's wolves turned into ashes. Ammon looked at Goon showing his teeth while Goon crouched down, preparing for attack. I had a clear shot of Ammon's threat. we couldn't kill him, but it would've slowed him down.

Naobi appeared out of nowhere and stood in between Goon and Ammon. “That is enough!” she shouted. Goon backed away, followed by the pack. Ammon shifted into his human form, dressed in his silk shirt and pants.

I’m assuming only the gods can shift back wearing clothes, Anik said to my thoughts.

I’m sure that is the case, but Goon better not shift back because he will be as naked as the day he was born, I said.

You will stop this behavior. It isn’t unacceptable. Now, let’s return to Anubi before the gate closes, and we’re stuck here waiting on it to open again,” Ammon fussed.

“I’m not going back. What about that do you not understand? I’m not happy there,” Naobi said. Sadness filled Ammon’s eyes. I felt sorry for him.

“I will put Dash, his pups and Kaira in a faraway temple away from us,” Ammon pleaded.

“I’m not your soul mate. The bond has never been there. I loved you, but you didn’t love me. I found my true soul mate, and he lives here on earth where I shall remain.”

“Where is he? I will defeat him,” Ammon said to Naobi.

"Let me go, Ammon," Naobi begged. Ammon grabbed Naobi's arm, and Goon charged into him. Ammon shifted back into wolf form. They tussled around while I and the other wolves howled. Ammon bit Goon really hard then slung him into the wall, knocking the wall down. A bolt of lightning struck Ammon, causing him to howl out in pain.

"That is your son! You will not attack him like he is your opponent," Naobi spat. Ammon shifted back then slowly pushed himself off the floor.

"My son needs to obey orders!"

"He has a right to protect his mother. You are not allowed to touch what doesn't belong to you."

It didn't take long to figure out that Naomi was the strength behind Ammon; she was the real power. Ammon knew without Naobi's power, he would be just a wolf god with nothing to stand behind him.

I licked Goon's wound on his shoulder as it closed up, and he growled at Ammon.

"You are turning my pup against me. I will respect your wishes. The gate is ready to close, but this isn't over, Naobi. We mated for life. I will defeat the man you bedded with. I can smell him on you. I will kill him, and you, my queen, will return home where you belong, sitting next to me. This is far from over," Ammon said then walked out of the house.

I looked around our home, and it was in the worse condition I have ever seen it in. Then a few seconds later, it was back to how it was. I looked at Naobi, and she winked at me. It looked as if Ammon had never come with his wolves that he didn't show any care for. Naobi kissed Goon's forehead then ran her fingers through his mane.

"I will see you later," Naobi said then disappeared. Goon and I headed up the stairs. As soon as we got into our bedroom, we shifted back.

"I cannot believe what just happened," I said to Goon. Then he picked me up to kiss me.

"I'm glad your beast didn't jump in with Ammon and me. I never want you to fight when I have the strength do it for us."

"I wanted to rip his throat out," I said and he laughed.

"I know. That's why I told you what I just did."

"You think Ammon is going to come back?" I asked Goon.

"No time soon, but he will. In the meantime, let's finish what we started," he said, leaning me against the wall. My sex dripped, and a whimper slipped from my lips when he kissed my neck. I licked his lips then bit his chest. "UMPH," Goon said as I bit him again. He held me up against the wall in our bedroom, his wide tip piercing through my opening. Every time he entered me, I felt like I was being ripped apart. My pussy gripped him tightly, and he groaned loudly. His canines bit into his lip. I arched my back away from the wall with only my shoulders leaning against it. He captured my nipple into his mouth and sucked firmly.

"GOOOONNNNNN," I called out to him. He rotated his girth inside of me, slowly grinding into my center as I dripped. He pulled himself out of me then entered me again, going deeper.

It gets very wet for me. I want to stay here all night, he said as I licked my lips. *Close your eyes, Kanya, and let me take you away."*

I slept peacefully in my bed until a scream came from downstairs. I hurriedly hid under my bed as heavy footsteps came up the stairs. I lay under my bed, covering my mouth to keep me from screaming. The intruder looked inside of my closet. My eyes followed the pair of Timbs that paced back and forth on my floor. I closed my eyes, hoping he would go away. I had a feeling he was going to kill me. All of a sudden, a pair of hands was pulling me from underneath my bed. My negligee rose up around my hips, exposing my purple lace thong. The masked intruder took his mask off, and blue eyes stared at me. Goon's hand traveled up my leg then around my hips. He ripped my panties off, spread my legs then eyed my swollen pussy. He howled when my nectar dripped onto the carpet. His clothes disappeared; he was naked. He pushed my legs all the way back then slid far inside of me. His testicles slapped against my bottom. Goon gripped my hair with one hand then covered my mouth with the other. I wanted him to fuck me so deeply. I wanted him to savagely ram himself inside of me. He heard my thoughts, and he pulled out then slammed into me again. My whimpers were muffled by his hand. My hips bucked forward meeting his hard, long thrusts. I clawed at his arm, scratching him as his big dick viciously slammed into my pussy, hitting my spot. I creamed heavily on him. The rug burned my back giving me extra pleasure. I lifted my legs up as high as they could go. Goon groaned then growled as his dick hardened, stretching inside of me. I rubbed my clit then smeared my wetness on his lips. He howled. The windows flew open, and the full moon shined on us. Sweat beads ran down my breasts and stomach while Goon slammed himself into my harder. A big wave came over me, and a breeze swept over my naked, damp body. My stomach tightened up, and then my clit swelled. Goon rubbed my clit, circling around it with his thumb. He knew what I wanted. He knew my clit throbbed to be touched. When Goon's dick got stuck inside of me against my spot, I howled louder than him as I had a climax that almost caused my chest to cave in…

"Open your eyes," Goon said, pulling out of me. When I looked around, we were standing in our room in the same spot. My legs shook, and my wetness was seeping from between my slit.

"You hypnotized me. You gave me a vision. It felt so real," I said to him, trying to catch my breath.

"I was inside of you. The pleasure was still real, just not how it happened," he chuckled.

"Warn me next time. I thought someone was going to rape me or kidnap me. I felt like I was in a horror movie." I said, walking into the bathroom. I ran the shower water then stepped in. Goon stepped in behind me. I couldn't wait to carry his last name. I was going to be Mrs. Uffe.

Dayo

I no longer had thoughts of Keora. When I used to have thoughts of her, I felt like I was betraying my pack brothers. After I came back from hunting, I grabbed my sweatpants, which were lying across a tree stump, then stepped into them. I walked into the house, heading towards the kitchen to drink a pitcher of water. When I walked into the kitchen, there she stood. Anik's scent was driving me crazy. I smelled her everywhere. I even smelled her in my sleep. She wore a jogging suit; the pants clung to her round hips and meaty bottom. I licked my lips then fixed myself before she noticed my erection.

"Good-morning," she said to me, cutting up thick pieces of bear meat.

"Where is everyone at? They was just here," I said to her.

"Kanya and Goon are out with the pups and Arya. Amadi is with Jalesa, and Elle didn't mention where he was going. Izra and Adika said they were going up in the mountains for a few days." Her jacket was unzipped, showing the right amount of cleavage. Her breasts looked more appetizing than a fat, juicy pregnant cow. I wanted so badly to suck them until she creamed on my dick. I hurriedly drank my water then left out of the kitchen. I didn't want to look at her that way. Anik was a young wolf; she was like a sister. I went into the gym room to blow off some steam, but I could feel her presence.

"What do you want, Anik? I'm busy."

"Why don't you say much to me? You know, flirt with me like how Goon does with Kanya or Izra does with Adika?"

"You're not my type. I don't look at you that way," I said to her while I did push-ups.

"Why not?"

I stood up. "Would you stop nagging me? I don't know why. Maybe because I just don't."

"Kanya was right; you are an asshole."

"Fuck Kanya. Don't tell Goon I said that neither." Anik walked away from the door, and I followed her. "Come here Anik!" I called out to her. She stopped walking. When she turned around, her eyes were watery. "What is going on?" I asked her.

"I feel something for you. When I try to stop it, I can't. I feel connected to you, and I'm pissed because I feel something for you, and you feel nothing," she said wiping her eyes. "I don't mean to be emotional, but my body hasn't been the same since I came here. I was wondering if I go away then so will the feelings I have for you."

My cell phone rang inside of my pocket; it was a woman that I had run into a few days before. I was at the mall in the shoe store, and the store clerk and I switched cell phone numbers. I hit the decline button, and then a text came through telling me she wanted to see me. When I looked up, Anik's eyes turned into slits; she was past angry.

"Well, I'm sure it's one of your human whores that you lust for all the time. You have a problem with your own kind. Why is that?" Anik asked me.

"Our kind mate forever. When you go into heat, it's because your body is ready to carry pups. I'm not ready for all of that shit. I want to be a free wolf and do as I please," I said to her, and then she walked out of my face. The sway of her hips and the way her bottom bounced when she walked away had my attention until my phone beeped again. Christiana texted me again. I called her back.

"Hellllooooooo," she sang into the phone.

"What's up? Are you free tonight?" I asked her.

"No, I will be busy tonight."

"What are you calling me for? I thought you wanted to see me. I see that you are into cat and mouse games, huh?"

"There's nothing wrong with a little chase. It makes it quite interesting, don't you think?"

"Be ready by nine. Send me your address," I said to her then hung up. I walked up the stairs then down the hall. I stopped when I heard moans coming from Anik's room. I crept to her door; she didn't shut it all the way. I peeked into the crack. Anik lay on her bed naked while she touched her pussy. Her legs were spread, and her sex permeated the air, seeping through the crack in the door. Her scent filled my nostrils.

Dayoooooooo! Anik moaned inside of her head. She wanted me to mate with her. A howl almost escaped my throat, and beads of sweat formed on my forehead. My dick grew, straining to burst out of my pants. Anik's nipples pointed straight up in the air. She moaned louder when she grabbed her breast and squeezed her nipples. Her middle finger entered her hole and gripped it tightly. Anik's pussy was very tight and untouched. My nails sharpened, and my fangs expanded from out of my gums. My beast wanted to come out; he wanted to penetrate her. My stomach cramped. Anik's scent was driving me crazy. Her back arched off the bed, and she moaned loudly as her legs shook. Her wetness ran down her leg. I felt something wet run down my leg. When Anik came, I came with her. I hurriedly went into my room before she saw me. I took a shower then got dressed in a pair of jeans, a hoodie and Nikes then rushed out of the house. Goon, Kanya and the pups pulled up.

Goon got out of his Suburban truck. “You act like you saw a ghost. Keora isn’t messing with you, is she?” Goon asked me. I peeked around him to see what Kanya was doing. She was getting the twins out of their carriers. Arya helped Kanya with the diaper bags. I didn’t want Kanya to hear me talk to Goon.

“Block Kanya from your thoughts real quick,” I said to him.

“What’s up? Why are you sweating?” Goon asked, smirking.

“Bro, Anik is in heat, and I watched her touch herself. Her scent is messing with me. I cannot do shit without thinking about her. I don’t want any pups or a mate right now.”

“Your ancestors saw visions of you with her. That is your mate, bro. There isn’t nothing you can do about that. I didn’t want to mate neither, but you cannot escape it. If she fuck another wolf, you will be far from the happiest wolf in the house.”

“I would like to know what ancestor saw visions of this shit so I can kick his old ass! We are still young wolves, bro. Anik is young. Her wolf hasn't even finished growing yet. She ain't that much bigger than Arya's wolf."

"Stop making up excuses," Goon said. I waved him off. I walked towards my motorcycle then put my helmet on.

"I will be back later. If Anik leaves the house, let me know," I told Goon as he walked up the steps.

"I'm not telling you shit!" he called out. I growled at him as I revved up my engine then took off down the long driveway. I didn't have a destination; I needed to kill time until Christiana got off from work.

*****

Hours later…

I pulled up in front of the address Christiana gave me. I hopped off my bike then walked through the fence. I knocked on the door of the two-story home. A few seconds later, she opened the door. Christiana wasn't anywhere near as pretty as Anik, but her body had more curves than a race car track. Her breasts sat up nice and full. She had what human women call a weave on her head. Her hair came down to her hips, and her skin was the color of chestnuts. Her nose was round, and her lips were very full. She was dressed in a short miniskirt with a cut off shirt revealing her belly ring. On her feet were a pair of heels that reminded me of the shoes that the strippers wore.

“Hey, handsome,” Christiana said to me. She had a nice scent, strong enough to get me aroused.

“What’s up?” I asked, smirking. She opened her door, inviting me into her home. I looked around, and it was junky; she had clothes and books everywhere.

“Excuse my home. I have two other roommates who live here too,” she said. I sat down on her couch, knocking some books off. “Would you like something to drink?”

I want to know where he is taking me. I hope he isn’t a cheap-ass negro. He looks like he has a lot of money; his motorcycle is the top of the line, Christiana thought. I chuckled to myself because I already knew what I wanted to do with her. I was going to buy her a lobster dinner, fuck her till she passes out then leave and never talk to her again.

"Naw, I don't like drinking while riding my bike. But I would like for you to hurry up and finish getting dressed," I said to her.

"I am dressed. You don't like it?" she asked me.

I burrowed this outfit from Keisha. I knew I should've wore my see-through shirt with my glitter bra, Christiana thought.

"We are going out to eat. if I had known I was going to be entertaining a stripper, I would've grabbed more ones," I said to her and her face dropped.

"You are an asshole," she said to me. I only smiled.

If he wasn't so chocolate and sexy, I would've kicked him out of my house. I bet he has a big dick; the arrogant ones always do. Christiana licked her lips. She grabbed her jacket then swished her hips as she moved to the door, her skirt raised up. I licked my lips as thoughts of me bending her over entered my mind. I followed behind her. *I hope he grabs my ass,* Christiana thought. I slid my hand under her skirt, grabbing a handful; she didn't have on any panties.

"You live freely, don't you?" I asked her.

"You only live once," she said, walking out of the door.

An hour later, we were being seated. Christiana received a lot of stares because of the way she was dressed.

"Good evening and thank you for dinning in with us tonight. What can I start you two off with?" the waiter asked us.

"Ummmm, I will take a Patron margarita and a shot of Patron straight on the side," Christiana said, scratching her hair. If I didn't know any better, I would've assumed she had fleas.

"What about you, sir?" the waiter asked me.

"A pitcher of water," I answered him. He wrote something down on his pad then walked off.

I hope he doesn't just order a salad and drink water because he doesn't have the money. That might not even be his bike," Christiana thought. I burst into a fit of laughter.

"What's so funny?" she asked me.

"I was just thinking about how funny it would be if I ordered all of this shit on this menu then walked out leaving you here," I chuckled.

"You wouldn't," she gasped, holding her chest.

"No, I wouldn't do that, but the thought was funny, but enough of that. When we leave here, what are we doing?" I asked, feeling on her leg. Her scent permeated the air; she was aroused. She wanted to be penetrated as much as I wanted to penetrate her.

"What do you want to do?" she asked, grabbing my erection under the table. Her eyes widened, and then her face dropped.

This can't be real. He is huge. I don't think he will fit, she thought.

"It gets bigger," I said to her. After her drinks and my water came, we ordered our food. I ordered a steak cooked rare with a potato. Christiana ordered stuffed lobster tail with crab meat, asparagus and scallops.

"Are you married?" she asked me.

"Don't you think that should've been asked before we got this far? My kind doesn't marry anyway," I said to her.

"What kind is that?"

"People who live freely, explore the world and run loose," I answered her. I was getting bored with her; she no longer piqued my interest. After our food came, I ate in silence while she ordered another lobster then dessert. Once the tab came, I paid then left a generous tip.

Maybe he is a drug dealer. He seems a little thuggish, she thought.

When we got back to her place, we ended up straight in her room. She took her clothes off, and her body was beautiful. Her breasts were nice and perky. I reached out to grab them, but Anik's full, round breasts popped into my head along with her thick thighs spread apart as she pleasured herself. She was all I could think of. Her wet sex glistened from thoughts of me, making her cum.

Christiana grabbed my dick, bringing me back to reality. She unzipped my jeans, pulling them down. When she got my dick out, she held onto it with two hands.

He is big, long and heavy, she thought. She opened her mouth, taking me in. Her mouth was warm and wet. The way she wrapped her mouth around me felt like pussy.

"Damn, Anik," I said, pushing myself further into her mouth.

"ASSHOLE!" Christiana yelled, standing up.

"What is your problem?" I asked her.

"Who is Anik?" she asked me with her arms crossed. I fixed myself then zipped up my pants. I fastened my belt then walked out of her room. She grabbed her robe then followed me downstairs.

"So, you are married?" Christiana asked me.

"Call me later," I said to her, walking out of the door then towards my bike. Christiana followed me outside.

"What is wrong with you? You call me another woman's name then leave me hot and fucking bothered? You have lost your everlasting mind!" Christiana shouted at me. I put my helmet on then revved up my engine. I gave her the peace sign then zoomed off, leaving her on the curb. I needed to hunt to clear my mind. I needed to figure out what I needed to do. Goon was right; no matter what I did, Anik was on my mind. She is my mate, and it was time for me to mate with her.

Goon

Kanya's voice yelled into my head asking me where I was at, but I didn't respond. I sat in my truck across from Kanya's parents' house. It was eight in the morning, and I knew her father was going to be leaving out for work. He walked out the house moments later wearing his suit with his coffee in one hand and his suitcase in the other. He walked like he was a big man, but he wasn't. He could probably ride on Arya's back when she shifted into her small beast.

I got out of my truck. "Jeffrey," I called out to him. He turned around with a scowl on his face.

"Come any closer and I will call the police."

"I don't care about that. I drove four hours to have a man to man talk with you."

"Make it quick. I have a meeting in a few hours, and New York traffic is a pain in the ass."

“I know you don’t like me for your daughter, but I love her. I’m going to marry her, and we will be together for eternity. We will be together when you are old and gray, dying on your death bed. You can think the worst of me, but I don’t care about that. All I care about is Kanya’s feelings. I hate to see her cry. When she is hurt, it hurts me. I came here to ask you…naw, fuck that. I came here to tell you that you will give her away to me next week. You will walk her down the aisle, and you will make her happy.”

“Listen here, convict. You will not come to my home and tell me what to do. I do not want my daughter with you in that house full of ignorant criminals. I do not feel safe with my grandsons in that house. You have illegal dogs in your home that eat deer like they’re kibbles and bits. You have a lot of expensive jewelry, a big house and expensive cars with no education. Izra is just as dumb as they come, and my daughter is wrapped up in your mafia. I will not give her away to you. I washed my hands of Kanya. No daughter of mine that had a proper upbringing will let some young-minded bastard screw her life up,” he seethed.

My fangs expanded, my eyes changed color and I felt my face growing out into a snout. Jeffrey dropped his coffee and suitcase.

"You will be there or else I will hunt you down. I will tear into your scrawny ass like a baby deer. But first, I will sink my fangs into your neck then snap it. If Kanya sheds one damn tear at our wedding because you didn't come, you can kiss your beautiful wife good-bye," I said to him as his body trembled. I backed away, and then he fainted. I chuckled then walked to my truck. When I got in, I pulled off.

"Where the hell have you been? You didn't respond to me in your thoughts or my calls!" Kanya said to me when I walked into the house.

"I was busy," I said as my pack brothers snickered.

"Goonie is in troubbllllleeeeee," Izra told Adika. Kanya's cell phone rang, and she walked away to answer it.

Arya sat at the kitchen island, drawing. I ruffled her hair. "Stop it, Uncle Goon," she said giggling.

"What are you drawing?" I asked her.

"We are working on mythical creatures. I'm drawing Medusa," she said. Arya attended school with the rest of the human kids. Pups her age are very vicious; they attack any and everything, but Arya was different. Maybe it was because she was from the Chippewa tribe, or it was because she picked up Anik's personality.

"How do you like your school?" I asked Arya.

"I like it. I have a lot of friends already. I told them I was having a sleepover," she said.

"A sleepover with a bunch of human kids? Not going to happen."

"I will ask Kanya," Arya said.

"I will bite the hell out of Kanya if she invites any more humans into our home," I said chuckling.

Kanya walked into the kitchen and started dancing. "My father is coming to our wedding. I feel so complete now," Kanya said, throwing her arms around me then kissed my lips.

"That's what's up, beautiful. What did he say?" I asked curiously.

"He apologized for the way he has been treating me, and he said that although he didn't approve of you, he was willing to try. It's going to take time for him to come around, but him even trying is good enough for me," she smiled. I kissed her forehead.

"Ughh get a room," Arya mumbled.

*****

One week later…

"Are you nervous about getting married?" Elle asked me. The wedding was only an hour away. I let Kanya and her human associates handle the wedding plans. Werewolf matings are stronger than any human marital tradition, but I knew it would make Kanya happy.

"Naw, I be happy to get this over with though. I didn't know Kanya knew a lot of humans. She invited people from high school and her old jobs," I said to Elle.

"You was going to get married without sending me an invitation?" a voice said from behind me. When I turned around, Kofi was standing behind me in his silk garments and his heavy medallion around his neck. I knew Ammon was my father by blood, but in my spirit, Kofi is my father.

Kofi reached out to me then hugged me. He pulled the rest of the pack into his embrace.

“Come on, old man. Don’t get emotional on me,” Izra said to him.

“I feel like I left a huge part of me when I went back to Anubi. I had all of you since you were young wolves,” Kofi said then looked at Dayo, patting his shoulder. Kofi never got a chance to see Dayo when Dayo came back from Keora’s prison. That was his first time seeing him in a long time. “Are you and Izra behaving?” Kofi asked him.

“He aight,” Izra said.

Dayo growled at Izra. “Take him to Anubi with you.”

“Amadi, you are glowing. How come?” Kofi asked him, smirking.

“Amadi been getting some magical pussy,” Izra said and Dayo snickered.

"Don't speak that way about Jalesa. She and I have not become intimate yet," Amadi said with his eyes turning in anger.

"Wait a minute, bro. You take her out on dates. You feed her fruit, massage her body and spend so much time with her that you're barely in the house, and you mean to tell me that you aren't giving her the beast? No biting? No howling? None of that?" Dayo asked Amadi.

"Mature wolves cater to their mates before they become intimate. You show them the nature of beast, and then when you make intimate love with them, they know how to accept him. You make love to her mind first, and she will forever be grateful," Elle said, making Kofi smile.

"I taught you well," Kofi said to Elle.

"I want you all to meet someone. I will be right back," Kofi said, walking out of the library in our home. Our wedding was going to be in the backyard. Kanya wanted an old-fashioned wedding. Kofi came back into the library with his mate. She looked just like Kanya but more mature. She had long braids with gold beads at the end. Her gold and turquoise dress wrapped around her body, hugging her voluptuous figure. She bowed her head to me because I'm the son of Ammon.

"This is Opal. She is my feisty little jackal. She is an ancestor to Kanya," Kofi said to us.

"This is the pack that kept me from my mate for years? What remarkable warriors you made them into. I can see in their structure that you taught them well," Opal said in her deep, distinctive accent.

"You look just like your father. He speaks very highly of you. One day, you will be the wolf god of Anubi," Opal said to me.

She reached into her sack then pulled out yellow diamonds and rubies. "My gift to you," she said then handed them to me. In Anubi, jewelry didn't mean anything; they gave it away freely. On earth, our ancient jewelry was worth a lot of money. At the bottom of our house, there was a mine of all of our jewelry that our ancestors left to us.

Kanya walked into the room. "I thought humans couldn't see their mate before the wedding?" Elle asked her.

"We aren't human," Kanya said in her black lace gown. She had real black diamonds around the neckline. The tail of her gown was eight feet long. Her hair was styled into some type of curls. I wasn't too fond of that hairstyle, but nevertheless she looked beautiful. Kanya looked at Opal. "You are Kofi's mate? I know so much about you. He always talked about how feisty you were."

Opal hugged Kanya. "It's so peaceful here. No wonder Kofi was getting homesick in Anubi."

"He was homesick here. Kofi doesn't know what he wants," Izra stated.

"We have not met your pups yet," I said to Kofi.

"My pups are older with pups of their own, and they have pups. I haven't seen them in years. Pups don't stay around their parents long when they age. They leave and we never see them again," Kofi said.

"Kanya, darrrrliinggggggg, there you are. Jessica is ready to do your make-up. Adika and Anik are finished. Now, lets hurry. The wedding is in a hour. Hey, everyone," Anastasia said, peaking his head into the door. Kanya excused herself then hurriedly rushed out of the room with her long dress trailing behind her.

"What is that? Why is she dragging her clothes that way?" Opal asked confused.

Kofi chuckled. "I will tell you about the traditions here later, but in the meantime, let me go and check to see if my orchestra music is still in my room," he said, pulling Opal behind him.

"Kofi thinks he's slick. He is about to get him some jackal pussy," Izra said. We all burst into a fit of laughter.

"If you hear a howl, then you know what that means," I said. Dayo started sweating. He took off his suit jacket and shirt. He sat down on the chair by the desk.

"I need some water," Dayo said with his eyes turning and his canines expanding from his gums. Elle hurriedly rushed off to get Dayo some water.

"What's going on?" Amadi asked him.

"Anik is in heat, and this dumb-ass will not mark her. He is starting to go into spells just like her. When it's time for a wolf to mate, there is nothing you can do to stop it. You better not mess up those pants. Kanya will have a howl if she sees everyone dressed the same but you," I said to Dayo.

"I think it's too late for that," he said, feeling embarrassed.

"Nigga, you just let one off in a room full of people? Don't tell me Anastasia made you feel a certain way. See I knew this nigga was gay," Izra said.

Dayo got up then punched Izra, and Izra flipped over the couch. When Izra got up, he leaped over the couch in mid-air, kicking Dayo in the mouth. Amadi and I pulled them apart.

"Get that piece of shit away from me before I kill his ass. You got one more time brother to offend my tradition, and I will bite your damn neck in your sleep," Dayo said, pulling away from us. Izra chuckled then walked out of the room. "That punk-ass muthafucka talk too much shit." Dayo banged on the desk, and it caved in under the pressure.

"Calm down, bro," Amadi said to him. Elle came back with two pitchers off ice-cold water. He dumped one on Dayo while Dayo drank the other one.

"Her scent is all over the place. Every time it gets stronger, I mess up my pants," Dayo said.

*****

The Wedding…

Kanya walked down the aisle with her father escorting her. Jeffrey looked nervous. When he looked at me, I smirked then nodded my head. Jeffrey almost lost his footing, but Kanya caught him before he fell. Stephanie wiped her eyes as Kanya and her father continued to walk down the aisle. My pack brothers stood behind me. Dayo wore black jeans instead of black dress pants. Jalesa, Adika and Anik stood on the other side wearing dresses similar to Kanya's, but theirs were shorter.

You look handsome. My mother's voice came inside of my head. I looked in her direction where she sat next to Kofi and Opal.

Thank you. I like your hair like that; it fits you. Did you get that necklace I sent to you? I responded.

Yes, I got it and I cherish it. When you was a little boy in your past life, you made me many, and I kept them all."

I had to learn from Kanya and her mother about wedding traditions. The pastor began to speak as Kanya and I stared at each other. After we exchanged our vows and rings, he told me to kiss her.

*****

"Are you sure the pups will be okay with the pack for that long?" I asked her in the back of our limo. We were going on our honeymoon to Africa. Kanya wanted to know about her roots. That's why we were also going to see Egypt.

"Yes, have a little more faith, Goon. The store and our pups will be fine for two weeks," Kanya said.

"That's a long time, Kanya."

"Don't worry. Elle will not let anything happen," she said, rolling up the partition. She gulped her champagne down, then took off her dress. She climbed on top of me with a short, black lace dress on that pushed her breasts up.

"What is this? Why is it so tight?" I asked her.

"It's a girdle; it holds in my unwanted fat."

"I want it," I said, ripping it off. Her hand grabbed my dick, and I growled.

"I always wanted to do it in a limo," she said, unzipping my pants."I was so wet when I saw you standing there in your tuxedo," she slurred. Kanya was drunk. She even managed to smoke a blunt with Adika and Izra. Before I knew it, her wet sex slid down onto my dick. She ripped my shirt, and her hair grew out into her wild mane that was almost the color of her jackal. Her canines expanded, and she put three long scratches on my chest. She leaned forward, bucking her hips on me. Her teeth clamped down on my neck.

"ARRGGHHHHHHHHHHHH! FUUCCKKKKK!" I said as she continued to ride me. I howled, and the limo swerved.

"Sshhhhhh," Kanya whispered into my ear as she bounced up and down on me. After she orgasmed, I was behind her, and she snuggled into me.

"Are we going to live happily ever after?" she asked me slurring, and I smirked.

"For eternity, beautiful," I said to her.

Dayo

I crouched down as I watched the deer move around in the woods. Just when I was about to attack it, Anik's wolf leaped onto it. She sank her teeth into its neck, rolling around on the ground with it. The deer kicked wildly as Anik cut off its air supply. Once the deer stopped moving, she let it go. She kneeled down over it, praying for her kill. After she was done, she tore into the deer.

I know you saw me ready to kill it, I said to her inside of her thoughts. She looked at me then growled, showing me her sharp canines. Blood dripped from her mouth and covered her face.

That's your problem, Dayo. When you want something, you have to hurry up and catch it. If you don't, someone else will, Anik's voice said followed by a few growls.

I sat and watched her eat. When she was finished, I licked her face, cleaning it off. Once I was finished licking her face, I ran off into the woods. I smelled another deer and I needed to eat.

After I ate, I took a shower and lay across my bed naked. Anik's scent tickled my nostrils. I growled deeply. My dick swelled and it ached. I put on a pair of sweatpants then walked down the hall where she slept. I sniffed by her door, and her arousal became stronger; Anik was pleasuring herself. She called out to me in her thoughts. My body temperature rose as I heard her moan, and a low, sexy growl came from her. Then she whimpered. I turned away from her door, but her scent pulled me back. I turned the knob, and her door opened. Anik was sprawled out on her bed with her pussy dripping. Her face looked like it was etched in pain. I took off my pants then climbed on top of her. Her eyes popped open in response.

"What are you doing?" she asked me, trying to cover herself up. I moved her hand and sniffed the hand she used to please herself with. I placed her fingers inside of my mouth, tasting her. She tasted better than she smelled. I hungrily took her swollen breast into my mouth, satisfying my craving for her, and she trembled underneath me. My dick was pressed against her wet center. Anik's pussy was drenched. As much as I wanted to enter her at that moment, I couldn't. I wanted to explore the wolf I have been craving. Anik panted when I pulled her nipple into my mouth with my teeth and arched her back. A growl escaped my throat; my beast wanted to come out. Anik moaned then whimpered as her trembling hands slid up my solid arms then to my chest. I slid down her body, kissing her. Seconds later, her pussy was staring at me. I spread Anik's legs then traced my tongue around her clit. Her nails grew, scratching my back.

"OOOOHHHHHH," she moaned out. When my tongue dipped into her tight, leaking hole, Anik growled loudly. My head thrashed around her pussy as my tongue hungrily explored her wet slit. Her tight hole clenched as her legs shook. *Dayyoooooooo!* she screamed inside of her head. I pinned her legs back, kissing her swollen bud. More of her wetness seeped, running down her ass. Her scent was getting stronger. My canines grew out, my breathing sped up, and my dick slowly leaked with my sperm. I kissed the inside of her thighs as I worked my way back up. Anik's eyes were goldish-brown with a hint of yellow in them. Her lips darkened to the same color as her beast lips. I was ready to enter her. I slowly entered her, but her hole was too tight; she tensed up.

It hurts, Anik's voice said. I started to pull away from her, but she pulled me closer. *I need it, please,* she begged.

I kissed her neck then bit her. My teeth sank into her neck as my dick slowly went further into her. A tear slid out of her eye as I marked her, and her body almost shifted. Her wolf hairs pierced through her skin, but then they went away. I was inside of her. My head spun. Anik felt better than any woman I have ever been with. Visions of her giving me pups entered my head. I slowly pumped inside of her; she was accepting me. She no longer felt pain. Her legs wrapped around me, and I pinned her legs back. I looked down and watched her tight pussy grip my swollen dick. My veins thickened, and her pussy gripped me tighter. Then I howled louder than my beast has ever howled. I sped up as Anik's creamy essence coated my dick. Her loud moans filled the room. I pulled out then slammed back into her. I fit inside of her perfectly. I groped at her breasts as I pumped into her, and the headboard slammed against the wall. Anik cried out in pleasure when I hit her pleasure spot. Her eyes rolled in the back of her head as her locks shook. I pulled out of her, my dick dripping with her fluids and mine. I turned her over.

Bend over and arch your back. She nervously did what I told her to do. Her Chippewa markings covered her lower back in red ink that was etched in her skin; she was unique. I spread her then entered her again. My beast's claws put three long scratches across her back as I pumped into her. I gripped her hips, bringing her onto my throbbing dick. Her pussy squeezed me, and I howled again. I pinned Anik down beneath me. My dick repeatedly jabbed her spot over and over again until her body collapsed. My head swelled inside of her, and then I exploded, my semen shooting into her.

"GGGRRRRRRRRRRRRRRRRRRRRRR!" I hollered out. Then I fell on top of her. Although Anik was in heat, her body wasn't ready to carry my pups. She had the urge for sex; the next full moon she will have insatiable desires and very strong urges, and I will fulfill them as her mate.

I helped Anik into the shower and then stepped in with her. She was quiet as the water ran down her body.

"Will the human whores you sleep with go away?" she asked, looking up at me as my body towered over hers. I kissed her.

"I'm done fighting it, Anik."

"So, you will not call me your little sister?" She traced her fingers down my chest and abs. *His build is so beautiful and strong,* she thought.

I chuckled. "After I just made your body respond to mine that way? I don't think so," I said to her.

*****

The next day…

"You sure was making a lot of noise last night," Elle said to me in the gym room.

"He marked Anik. She walked past me this morning smelling just like Dayo's beast," Amadi said, doing push-ups.

"Get ready, Dayo. She is going to be going through spells until she is ready to get pregnant. When she gets those cramps, run and never come back," Elle joked. I sat up on the weight bench.

"What cramps?" I asked Elle.

"The cramps that make her bleed. Her body is preparing itself to carry your pups for two months. Her uterus will grow before she gets pregnant, preparing her for the pups that will grow at a rapid rate inside of her womb," Amadi said.

"Where did you two come from? I know we've been around for years, but you two are stuck," I joked.

"I'm just preparing you, that is all. Goon almost ran for the hills, and he doesn't crack under anything. But I know you, and you will not be able to handle it," Elle said while Amadi chuckled.

My phone rang, and it was a human woman that I had bedded in the past. I answered the phone. “What’s up, Keisha?” I asked.

I heard a baby crying in the background. “Dayo, I need you to come and see your daughter,” she said to me.

“Excuse me?” I asked her.

“You been avoiding me for months! I had a baby, and she is only a few weeks old. You need to come and see about her!” Keisha said into the phone.

“I’m not the father, and besides, you are a human. You would be dead if you gave birth to my pup,” I said into the phone as Amadi and Elle laughed with tears in their eyes.

“What on earth did you just say to me? Are you on drugs?”

“Keisha, I’m not the father, and I would appreciate it if you didn’t call me anymore. My mate wouldn’t approve of that; wolves are very territorial beasts,” I said, making Elle and Amadi laugh even harder.

“I’m taking you down for child support!” she screamed then hung up the phone.

"Bro, what kind of human women do you bed with?" Amadi asked me.

"Hoodrats," I said to them. Elle and Amadi looked at me curiously.

"They have rat shifters?" Elle asked me.

"What kind of shifter is a hoodrat?" Amadi asked me.

"Its slang for women that are sluts. You know, jezebels," I said to them.

"Human language in this generation is complicated," Elle said, walking out of the gym room.

*****

Amadi, Elle, Izra, Adika, Jalesa and I all sat around a fire in the woods. Akea and Kanye were in Adika's lap sleeping peacefully. Arya and Anik did some type of spirit dance; they were celebrating the lives of the wolves that were killed in their tribe. Anik wore a two-piece, suede outfit. She had paintings on her face. Anik and Arya both had their hair parted in the middle with two long braids hanging down on the side. Around her feet were squirrel tails that were hooked onto a bracelet. Anik and Arya danced, making noises. I smiled because Anik was free-spirited. Her hips swayed side to side, and she moved seductively as her eyes were trained on me.

If I would've known you could move like that, I would've marked you sooner, I said inside of her thoughts.

You are an asshole, she replied.

I'm your asshole, I said back.

Naobi

I walked into the basement with a tray of food for Keora, who lay in her cell. It was almost like a human prison; she had a toilet and a shower. I had clean clothes draped over my arm for her. I sat the tray down by her cage.

"When are you letting me out of here?" Keora asked me.

"Not until you find yourself. I can still sense the evil inside of your soul. When I feel that you are ready, I will recreate you. But I refuse to do so while you are this way," I said to her.

"What do you want me to do?" Keora cried.

"I want you to think of all you have done. I want you to think about how you hurt me, my son, Akea and your sister, Adika. I saw everything you have done, and I'm disgusted. I feel nothing for you, my child, until you find yourself," I said to her then walked out of the basement. I went into my sanctuary that I had inside of Kumba's home. I locked the door then sat on my rug. I had a few globes in front of me. In one globe, Akua and Kanya toured Egypt on their honeymoon. They were happily in love. It warmed my heart as I watched Akua gaze lovingly into Kanya's eyes. The other globe I had was of Anubi. I was no longer in their world, but I still felt and saw their visions. Dash was training to become a warrior. Kofi and Opal fed each other grapes and raw meat. Kaira and Ammon were mating as Ammon howled out. Once he was finished, he sent her away, and she left out of his room obediently. Ammon was thinking about me; he missed me. I felt his rage. He wasn't going to let me go. Ammon wanted to fight for me; he wanted me to come back home.

Ammon got dressed in his gold garments then went into the far end of his temple. He knocked on Musaf's door. Musaf opened the door…

"I need a favor from you. I need you to make my warriors stronger. I need to bring my mate back to Anubi where she will sit next to me on my throne," Ammon said to Musaf.

"If I do a favor for you, you must do one for me," Musaf said in his language.

"What is that?"

"After the year is done, I will no longer be able to have offspring. I need a witch who can carry my seed in her womb. This new offspring shall be more powerful than all of my others," Musaf said very lowly. He rarely talked, but when he did, it was like a whisper.

"Witches can't carry in their womb."

"Yes, one can. Jalesa was born human but reincarnated by Naobi. She can carry my seed in her womb."

"I will bring you Jalesa if you make my warriors stronger," Ammon said.

I heard the door upstairs shut. I sat my globe down. I went upstairs to greet Kumba.

"How was your day?" I asked him before he leaned down to kiss me. I needed to warn the pack. Ammon was going to take Jalesa away from Amadi. Ammon wasn't going to stop until I returned back to Anubi. He was going to create a war between Anubi and the immortals on earth, and he didn't realize it. Ammon didn't love me; he loved power. I was the strength behind him, and without me, he felt like he couldn't rule as the wolf god.

Beauty in the eyes of his Beast: The pack (Spinoff)

Made in United States
Orlando, FL
15 March 2023

31044717R00204